DARK SHADOWS: VAMPIRES AND GHOSTS OF NEW ORLEANS

AUTHORS ON A TRAIN VOLUME ONE

MOLTEN
UNIVERSE

Edited by Zach Bohannon and J. Thorn

Proofread by Eve Paludan

Cover by Elderlemon Designs

INTRODUCTION

On a brisk November evening, a group of bleary-eyed authors meets at the train station in Chicago. Although that's not the setup to a joke, it could have been. Getting on a train in a strange city with writers you've never met to spend a week in New Orleans working on a short story collection seems like an impossible challenge.

"Authors on a Train" was coined when Joanna Penn (aka J.F. Penn) jokingly hashtagged a Tweet during that first experimental trip in March of 2017. Zach and I went to New Orleans with Joanna and Lindsay Buroker to co-write a novella set in the *American Demon Hunters'* world. We survived the week and successfully published *American Demon Hunters: Sacrifice* just a few weeks later. While on that trip and having a life-changing experience (both of us), Zach and I had a crazy idea: What if we hosted an experience like this for other authors? Why *tell* people how to creatively collaborate when you can *show* them? And as they say, the rest is history.

Our intrepid authors who gathered in the Amtrak lounge on the inaugural and official, "Authors on a Train" retreat had been getting to know each other in a private online group and through email, but none had met face-to-face. In fact, two of our attendees came from England, and one flew all the way from Sydney, Australia. And as soon as we'd boarded the 8:05 to New Orleans, the collaborations began. Our mission? Spend a week in New Orleans, immersed in the culture, while learning how to co-write and collaborate on a short story to be published in a New Orleans-themed collection, the very one you're holding in our hands right now. To some of the authors, and to us, at times, this appeared to be an unattainable goal.

Could we pull it off? Could these first-time collaborators craft a story with their partner, whom they'd never met, and submit a final draft to us just a few weeks later? Not only did they make it happen, but they also made it stellar. We could not be prouder of this elite group of creatives. Their life experiences and writing styles varied greatly, not to mention cultural, linguistic, and regional idiosyncrasies. And yet, the stories in this collection are incredibly rich, interesting, and cohesive.

For you, dear reader, how we did it is not relevant. You're looking for good stories, not a journalistic piece on the merits of co-writing. But it must be noted that this could not have happened without the support of dynamic companies like Kobo, Draft2Digital, Findaway Voices, Vellum, Story Grid, Literature & Latte, Symmetric Design, and BookFunnel. LaunchPad New Orleans provided us with a home away from home. And our old friend, Patrick from Amtrak, took care of us on the rails, and we're happy to say he is alive and well (a little inside joke for those who've read *Sacrifice*). I owe a debt of gratitude to the mentorship of Shawn Coyne as we applied fundamentals of *Story Grid* methodology throughout the pre-production and revision process. And without my partner in crime, Zach Bohannon, this experience wouldn't have happened at all.

I hope you'll agree that these stories are not only a triumph of the experience and a snapshot in time that we'll never forget, but they're *really* good stories. *Voodoo Child* opens the collection, a story about a sick girl, a voodoo charm, and an old woman whose name still makes folks in the French Quarter shiver. Next up is *The Casket Girls*, a "prequel" of sorts for fans of the *Final Awakening* series and exclusive to this collection. Readers told us they wanted more Casket Girls—we heard you. Rising from the ashes, *Phoenix* is a murder-mystery and New Orleans ghost story wrapped into one exciting tale. If multi-dimensions and mysterious witch doctors are more your speed, check out the romantic ghost story, *The Amulet*. And finally, *Blood Moon* closes the collection, a lighthearted and sensual spin on a classic vampire theme.

Molten Universe Media is thrilled to present, *Dark Shadows: Vampires and Ghosts of New Orleans (An Authors on a Train Short Story Collection)*. This collection represents all our hard work and creative magic drawn from the eclectic, raw, and always exciting French Quarter of New Orleans, Louisiana.

If you'd like to know more about what we did, how we did it,

or when we're doing it again, go to
http://authorsonatrain.com

J. Thorn (and with Zach Bohannon)
January 13, 2018

VOODOO CHILD

BY Ashley Lauren and Christopher Wills

So far, Sophie had been disappointed. Well, she had seen those creepy giant spiders, but Sophie had her heart set on seeing a ghost.

When she'd checked into the New Orleans Specialty Hospital of Stem Transplants, she had fully expected to see a translucent apparition or two. After all, the old plantation mansion house overlooking the Mississippi River was close to a large nineteenth-century cemetery and rumor had it that the ghosts of those buried in the cemetery wandered the hospital hallways.

Unfortunately, the closest thing she'd seen to a ghost was several people dressed in strange, out-of-date clothing. Women in long dresses, wearing huge hats and gloves and men decked out in old-fashioned, long-tailed coats occasionally passed her in the hallway or walked by her open door. She never saw any of them go through walls or do anything out of the ordinary. She'd even mentioned seeing a woman with an exceptionally crazy hat with what looked like a peacock feather to one of her nurses. The young nurse had laughed, commenting that the hospital attracted the strangest visitors.

"Take, for instance, the woman next door," the nurse had said. "She says she's a voodoo witch and she keeps a large rubber snake in her room." The nurse had shuddered slightly, and then she'd crossed herself and had asked Sophie if she needed anything else.

A real voodoo witch with a rubber snake? Sophie had to find out more. "A voodoo witch?"

Her nurse waved a hand. "Bless her heart. I shouldn't be spreading rumors and talking about guests."

"Patients," Sophie corrected. Sophie hated that everyone here tried to pretend that everything was okay. The ten patients in this small, ultra-expensive hospital were all desperate and most likely dying.

"Guests, Miss Sophie. You are my guest. Now, if you don't need anything else, I'll be going."

Denied any more information, Sophie bided her time until that evening. Sophie's evening nurse, Beatrice, was an older woman, with leathery skin that resembled a raisin. She wore at least five crosses around her neck and was always complaining about the chill in the old hospital. Beatrice had a soft spot for Sophie, claiming her sixteen-year-old granddaughter looked just like Sophie.

Sophie scoffed at that idea. They might be the same age, but Sophie doubted Beatrice's granddaughter was bald with sickly yellowed skin and sunken-in brown eyes.

When Sophie asked about the witch, Beatrice crossed herself and said, "Don't you bother yourself with the likes of Madame Laveau. I don't know about her being a voodoo witch, but it seems to me that she is pure evil. I've been around long enough to know evil when I see it, and on that woman, I can even smell it. I don't go into her room unless I have to. It gives me the creeps." She crossed herself again. "Miss Sophie, you stay clear of that woman."

Sophie wasn't scared, not much anyway. But she was intrigued. There was no way she was going to miss a chance to see a real voodoo witch.

So, at midnight, when most sensible people and patients were asleep, Sophie snatched her hat from the rolling IV pole near her bed and twirled it around a finger. Dad had given her the Indiana Jones style hat on her tenth birthday before she went in for her first stem-cell transplant. The transplant didn't work, but Sophie always kept her hat close to remind herself that adventure was to be found anywhere. At the moment, the possibility of seeing a voodoo witch beckoned to her. She dropped the hat onto her head and got out of bed.

Sophie found herself in front of an elaborate oak door, holding her IV stand and wearing her trusty hat. Sophie stopped a couple of yards short of the large oak door, not the kind she expected to see in a hospital. It looked like it had been installed when the building had originally been built, with spiraling patterns entwined in its faded, dark colors. The door added to the mystery of what she might find on the other side.

She didn't believe in voodoo, but now, she was about to come face to face with a voodoo witch. It was all make-believe and trickery for the tourists. What harm could some old voodoo witch do to her? Sophie was dying anyway.

She turned the handle, pushed the door, and entered. It was dark, but in the low lighting, she could see an old woman lying in bed.

The supposed witch was a tiny woman with light-brown

leathery skin, and black hair peppered with gray strands. She wore a yellow headscarf and large hooped earrings, and her face was heavily made up. If Sophie hadn't been told otherwise, the woman could have been someone's sweet grandmother.

Hanging beside the bed was a long, teal-blue, silk dress that wouldn't look out of place in a Mardi Gras parade. On the bedside table sat a small cotton drawstring bag, but the thing that caught Sophie's attention was the rubber snake. It seemed like a strange thing to have on the nightstand in a hospital room.

She had an odd compulsion to touch it. But if she let go of the door, it would shut, leaving the room in total darkness. Even so, it was tempting. Her hero, Indiana Jones, would have darted out of the room by now, but Sophie stood transfixed by the rubber snake.

She heard a gentle cough and looked right to see another person in the room. Next to the window stood an attractive, young black woman wearing a simple gray linen dress.

Sophie immediately mouthed the words "sorry" to the woman and turned to leave the room, disappointed she hadn't been able to touch the rubber snake.

"You can see me, miss?" asked the young woman.

Sophie turned back, whispering, "Of course I can. I'm not blind."

"It's just that—"

The witch in the bed gasped for air, her voice hoarse and dry. Sophie froze. She was waking up. A sinking feeling settled in Sophie's stomach, warning her of danger.

Sophie also saw fear on the young woman's face as the voodoo witch shifted in the bed. Sophie decided she should go. She stepped backward, and the wheels of her IV stand squeaked in protest. The witch sat up straight and looked at Sophie.

"Get her out of here," shrieked the witch in a rasping voice. "She'll ruin everything."

The witch scrabbled around on her bedside table for something. She finally grasped the cotton drawstring bag with her withered and twisted hand, but during the process, she'd disturbed the hideous rubber snake. The rubber snake came to life, raising its head above the coils and transfixing Sophie with its stare.

She heard the young woman shout, "Run!" but Sophie couldn't move. The snake's stare hypnotized her.

The witch pulled a handful of powder from the drawstring bag with her claw of a hand and threw the mixture of dirt, herbs, bits of sticks, and small bones across the room, sprinkling Sophie. Her wizened voice chanted foreign words, but they sounded ominous to Sophie's ears.

Sophie heard the young woman shout another warning, "Get outta here, girl!"

This time, Sophie was able to blink, breaking the snake's spell over her. She looked at the young woman for a second, and then turned and ran out of the room.

———

THE HEAVY WOODEN door swung shut, casting the room back into darkness. The young woman, Constance, flipped on Madame Laveau's bedside lamp, knowing it was expected of her.

"You stupid *domestique*," said Madame Laveau. "That girl could have killed me while I slept. Fine bodyguard you are."

The insults from the witch no longer hurt Constance as they used to. She had put up with them for a long time. Too long. And it wasn't her position to guard the woman; that was the awful snake's job.

"That waif of a girl is no threat to a powerful witch such as you, Mistress."

Constance saw the glare from her mistress. It was a familiar glare, but this time, there was something else in her eyes. It took Constance a moment to identify it. *Fear.* Madame Laveau was afraid of that frail girl with wide brown eyes. She had scared the witch. But how? Constance had never seen fear in the witch before.

Constance dropped her gaze, as was expected and resumed her position by the end of the bed, waiting for the next insult. She felt the witch's eyes on her for a few moments, and then the pressure eased.

The witch barked a command for her pet snake to sleep. The snake lowered its head and curled up. Then she patted about in her blouse until she found the charm tucked beneath the folds of cloth. It was a simple gold charm that held a lock of Constance's hair. It was the charm that tied Constance to the voodoo witch.

As the witch fingered the charm, Constance felt the familiar tug that pulled on her soul. It made her insides crawl, even after all these years.

The witch laughed. "Listen to me, *domestique*. I'm not dead yet and won't be for many years. You will continue to serve me while I hold this *gris-gris*. Do you understand?"

Constance didn't need reminding of who was in charge or how she was bound to this hellish witch. "Yes, ma'am. I understand."

But even though the *gris-gris* voodoo charm controlled her body and her will, Constance was still free to think. She was thinking about the girl. How could the girl see her? And what was it about the sick girl that scared the great Madame

Laveau? It was a mystery for sure. A mystery that needed to be figured out.

———

SOPHIE FELT SO ALIVE, practically flying through her hospital bedroom door. She had more energy than she had in months. She jumped onto her bed and began to giggle.

That crazy old woman really believed she was a voodoo witch, with her strange mechanical rubber snake, and the stuff she threw from that bag. What was that all about?

Only a little had landed on her, but there was no way Sophie was going to tell her mom about it. First, she'd have her sanitized from head to toes, as she was obsessed with cleanliness and germs, and second, she'd probably insist on the old witch being moved to another floor. Sophie didn't want the witch moved. She wanted to see that mechanical rubber snake again. How cool was that? She wanted one for her room.

Mom meant well and was just trying to help, but Sophie had spent most of her life trapped behind the walls of her home or in hospitals. Rules, regulations, and hundreds of medications on strict time schedules dictated her life. Sophie was tired of it all. None of it was making her better, not yet anyway. Tonight was different. Tonight, she had stood face-to-face with danger, even if it was only a rubber snake and an old woman. Sophie felt *alive*, like she was really living, not hampered by her latest medical treatment fed to her through a plastic tube.

She saw that her drip medication of painkillers, hanging from her IV pole, was three-quarters empty. Her nurse, Beatrice, would be around to check on her in another hour or two and renew her medication bag. If Sophie wasn't sound asleep, the nurse would inform her mom and dad she wasn't sleeping. Then, they'd be with her twenty-four hours a day, pestering her or convincing the doctors to add a sedative to her medication.

That would be the end of her adventures, and she still hadn't seen a ghost. A voodoo witch, maybe, but not a ghost. Sophie loved her parents, but one of the problems with being seriously ill was that her mom and dad, but mostly her mom, seemed to think she couldn't do anything for herself. Sophie enjoyed the small bit of freedom she had roaming the old hospital at night and looking for ghosts.

It was the most fun she'd had in years. She didn't blame her parents. She knew it was hard for them as well. Beatrice told Sophie that a parent's worst fear was to see their child die before them. Sophie could understand that, but her parents needed to be managed, otherwise they'd smother her. She had to live while she could, even if it was just a bit of ghost hunting. The treatments and medications weren't going to cure her; Sophie knew she was going to die.

WHEN SOPHIE WOKE, her mother and father were in her room. Mom got up from her chair and sat on the edge of Sophie's bed. Her long elegant fingers brushed along Sophie's cheek, and a brittle smile lit her face.

"You're finally awake. I'm so relieved." When Sophie just blinked, her mom continued, "You never sleep that deeply. I was concerned."

"I'm fine, Mom. Stop worrying."

"I will soon. The doctor should have the results soon."

Sophie had forgotten about the tests. She had long since given up on the endless treatments. She wanted to be cured, but the constant rounds of drugs and operations seemed to only weaken her.

Mom glanced back at Dad. He moved to the bed and offered Sophie a smile.

"It's mid-afternoon, kid. You've slept like the dead all morning."

Mom's face registered indignant horror. "For God's sake, Jonathan, show some tact."

"Sorry, darling."

Mom became distracted, rooting around in her handbag, and Sophie grinned at her dad. Sophie much preferred Dad's direct manner to her mom's tiptoeing around reality. Dad knew that there wasn't a miracle cure for cancer. Mom, on the other hand, ignored that fact, hence the long traipse around new and experimental treatments. If Mom even suspected that the witch next door could cure her, she'd be begging the woman for a voodoo cure and promising her own soul to evil spirits, if it would save her daughter.

Now, that would be something to see. Mom facing off with the witch. Sophie wasn't sure which one would win.

Sophie stretched, rolling her neck. She paused and blinked a few times. The constant companion of pain was gone. There were still some twinges of discomfort, but nothing like what she was suffering a few days ago, which was odd. Was it the thrill of the adventure last night or was the latest experimental treatment really working? Sophie wasn't sure, but she was going to live to the fullest while she could.

"The pain is a lot less lately, so I guess I was able to sleep in."

Dad smiled. "Now, that sounds like something you haven't done enough of in your teenage years."

Mom beamed. "See, I knew this treatment would be the one."

"Now, Kate, I know we are all hoping for some good news this afternoon, but let's hold off on the party balloons until we hear back from the doctor."

"I know, but I've had a good feeling about this place and the treatment ever since I read about it six months ago." Mom squeezed Sophie's hand and brushed at a stray tear rolling down her own cheek. "I just know the doctor will bring back good news."

Sophie had the same opinion as her father. She wasn't ready to declare herself cured, but the decrease in pain and a real smile from both her parents was something to celebrate. She leaned into her mother and gave her a tight hug and the lights in her room went out.

The afternoon sun still came in through the big window, but Sophie felt a chill run up her spine. This wasn't a good sign.

"What's happening?" asked Mom.

"I'm sure it's nothing. Old buildings like these are sure to have a few bugs in the wiring," Dad said. The lights flickered a few times and then came back on. "See, no problem."

A nurse popped into the room with a half-smile. "Sorry about that. The power went out, and it took a few seconds for the backup generator to turn on. But there's nothing to worry about."

Sophie's mom's eyes opened wide. "Is the power out everywhere? Are you sure you have enough fuel? Jonathan would be happy to run out and get more—"

Jonathan took her hand. "I'm sure the hospital has everything under control."

"Of course, sir. I'm sure the regular power will be back on soon, and if not, we have enough fuel to feed the generator for a week or more." The nurse gave Sophie's mom a reassuring smile and left.

Before any of them had a chance to make another comment, there was a knock at the door. The doctor entered, carrying a clipboard filled with a stack of papers.

"Mr. and Mrs. Rothschild?"

"Yes?" Sophie's parents replied in unison, moving toward the doctor.

"I've got the test results back."

"Yes?" Mom's voice rose an octave, and she encroached into the doctor's personal space, causing him to take a step backward.

The doctor fiddled with his wire-rimmed glasses, avoiding her mother's eyes. Without hearing the doctor's words, Sophie knew what the results revealed.

A long time ago, she had accepted that she was dying. It was only question of when. At times like this, she remembered what Father Brown had told her in the early days of her illness.

"We all start dying from the day we're born. Everybody dies. It's part of life. All we can do is to be the best person we can, help everyone we can, and have a little fun on the way. Even the good Lord won't deny us having a little fun."

Sophie liked that. She found ways daily to have a little fun and even occasionally find a bit of mischief.

The doctor glanced at Sophie and then quickly looked away. "I think it's best if we go to my office and discuss this."

Mom's face crumpled as she bit her lip so hard she almost drew blood. But when Mom turned to her, the expression had changed to her best, but highly worn-out, fixed smile. Sophie smiled back. Mom made a valiant effort to cross her fingers on both hands and raise them in the air as she followed the doctor out of the room. She was on the verge of breaking down completely.

Dad grinned at the hat perched on the IV pole. "Adventures come in all shapes and sizes." He gently kissed Sophie on the cheek and left the room.

A tear trickled down Sophie's cheek. Dad understood her. He knew that Sophie craved adventure and fun, but they both knew those days were over.

As SOON AS she was alone, Sophie thought about what she had seen in the room next door. If she only had a short time to live, she had to risk another look at the old witch, and she had to touch that snake. The mechanical rubber thing was creepy and looked real, though not as real as the spiders that came out at night in the hospital.

Sophie heard a distressed cry through the closed door, pulling her out of her thoughts. Mom's muffled sobs filtered through the thick door, and Sophie knew that she'd have to comfort her.

They came back into the room. Mom was wearing her 'I'm trying hard not to look worried face,' but the telltale red-rimmed eyes and the newly applied makeup gave her away. Dad's expression mostly hadn't changed, but Sophie could see the resignation in his eyes that wasn't there before.

Mom sat on the chair beside Sophie and put out her hand.

Sophie clasped Mom's hand. "Don't worry. Everything's going to be fine."

Mom leaned forward and buried her head into Sophie's shoulder. Sophie patted her mom's back and offered a small smile to Dad. He moved to them both and gathered his wife and daughter in his arms. Sophie closed her eyes and took a moment to hold on to the feeling of all of them close together. If there was an afterlife, Sophie wanted to remember this moment forever.

BEEP. BEEP. BEEP. A cacophony of echoing screeches blared out of the alarm attached to the ceiling.

Sophie's parents jumped back from the bed. The hospital room door was flung open, and a nurse entered.

"It's a fire alarm. Mr. and Mrs. Rothschild, you need to leave and follow everybody else."

"What about Sophie?" asked Dad.

"We have that covered." As she finished, another nurse came into the room with a wheelchair and a blanket.

"Can we help?"

"Thank you, Mr. Rothschild, but no. We have a practiced procedure, and you'd only get in the way."

"Okay. Come on dear, let them do their job." Dad led Mom out, but not before Mom offered Sophie a half-hearted smile.

Sophie sat in the wheelchair while one nurse efficiently moved her IV from the stand to a hook attached to the wheelchair. The other nurse wrapped the blanket around her and whisked Sophie out to the corridor. She saw the voodoo witch a few feet away from her.

The witch gave Sophie a nasty glare and mouthed something at her. Sophie couldn't make out what she'd said, but she could see from the witch's facial expression that it was something malicious. Feeling brave, Sophie narrowed her eyes at the old witch and stuck out her tongue. The old woman looked away. Sophie counted it as a small victory and attributed her bravery to the fact she knew she was going to die. She had nothing to lose. The old witch couldn't hurt her now.

Sophie held onto her smile as she was pushed to the top of the stairs and left for a moment. She saw a few of those strangely dressed people moving throughout the hall, darting around the rushing medical personnel. They weren't trying to exit the building. Was this some sort of fire *drill* instead of a real emergency?

Two large men came up the stairs. They each took a side of Sophie's wheelchair, lifting it up and carrying it down the two flights of stairs.

Sophie found herself with a nurse in the Stage 1 evacuation area, located in one of the courtyards outside the old plantation house.

"Are you okay, Sophie?"

"Fine, thanks."

"I've heard rumors this is a false alarm. I'll check it out and be back in a minute."

Sophie didn't mind being left alone. It gave her a chance to be outside and get some fresh air, a welcome departure from the stale hospital environment. She couldn't see her parents in the walled courtyard. The only person she saw was the young woman who had been in the witch's room.

The woman approached Sophie with slow, reluctant steps. She stopped in front of her, swaying slightly.

"Hello, miss."

Sophie raised her eyebrows. "Hello."

The woman leaned against the wall, taking deliberate deep breaths.

"Are you okay?" Sophie asked.

"You can see me?"

Sophie rolled her eyes. "Duh. I told you already. What are you, a ghost or something?"

"Yes, ma'am. I am a ghost."

"Yeah, right." Sophie tried to laugh, but a sudden chill swept by, and she pulled the blanket tighter around herself.

"Miss, if you don't mind me asking, where are your parents?"

The woman's eyes were darting around, and Sophie was beginning to feel uncomfortable around someone who served a witch. "I'm not sure. Why don't you go and find them for me?"

The woman offered Sophie a wink and then walked toward the wall. She didn't hesitate as she walked straight through the solid stone wall. Sophie barely managed to hold in her squeak of surprise when she reappeared in front of Sophie a moment later.

"Yes, miss. They're on the other side of that wall."

"But you... You...."

"I'm a ghost, and I can walk through walls."

Sophie gasped. First, a voodoo witch, and now, a ghost. She wished there were such things as ghouls and monsters. The last twenty-four hours had been more exciting than her previous sixteen years put together.

"Wow. That's amazing. Do it again."

"But, miss, will you hear me out, please?"

"Sure, but go through that wall again."

The ghost walked through the wall and back again. Sophie grinned. Her parents would never believe this. Well, maybe her dad would, but Mom would think Sophie's medication needed to be adjusted.

"My name is Constance, miss."

"Constance. It suits you. Would you please stop with the 'miss this' and 'miss that'? Call me Sophie."

"Yes, mi... Sophie. I am owned by the old woman in the room next to you."

"Owned? Like a slave?" Sophie asked.

"I ain't a slave. Madame Laveau is a voodoo witch, and she holds a *gris-gris* charm that makes me obey her. I need your help."

"Me? I'm just a teenage girl. What can I possibly do for you?"

Constance hung her head and sighed. "You're right. You can't help me." Constance turned to leave through the wall.

"Constance, wait. What do you want?"

"It could be dangerous."

Sophie leaned forward in her wheelchair. "You definitely have to tell me now."

"I needs you to get the *gris-gris* from the witch. If you can get it away from her, I will be freed."

"You want me to steal something?"

"Yes, but you needs to take care."

"I'm dying. How bad could it be? And why me?"

"You can see me and nobody else in 200 years has been able to do that. And Madame Laveau is afraid of you."

Why would an old woman be afraid of a young and weak girl?

"So, how do I get this *gris-gris* thing?"

Constance licked her lips and took a deep breath. "Tomorrow morning, at nine o'clock, the witch will be put to sleep and taken for surgery. She'll leave the charm with the snake."

"What charm? Is that what the *gris-gris* is?"

"The *gris-gris* is a charm the witch wears around her neck. It's got a lock of my hair in it. If you take my hair out of the charm, I'll be free."

Steal a charm from a mechanical snake and open it. Not exactly the Ark of the Covenant or the Holy Grail, but she could be Sophie, the adventurer who saved a ghost.

"I'll do it. Tell me about the rubber snake."

"It's not rubber. It's real and very poisonous. The thing is bound to the witch and must follow her commands. And it's not just the snake you need to worry about. There's danger from the witch herself."

Sophie narrowed her eyes at Constance. "I thought she was going to be in surgery?"

"She is. But you must not leave any part of yourself in the room. If you do, she will make a *gris-gris* for you, and you will be under her power for eternity. Not even one hair."

Constance paused, putting her hands over her face. "Oh, I'm sorry, miss. I didn't mean to..."

Sophie laughed. "I haven't got any hair, so no problem, right?"

Constance paced back and forth in the small walled courtyard. She stopped as if she had made a decision.

"No," said Constance. "I can't ask you to do this, Sophie. It's too dangerous."

Before Sophie could protest, Constance had disappeared through the wall, leaving Sophie alone. She wondered if she had imagined the entire conversation.

SOPHIE'S NURSE, Beatrice, collected her from the evacuation area. The fire alarm turned out to be a hoax. Someone had pulled it, sending the hospital into chaos. Beatrice was none too quiet in her opinion that the responsible individual should be banned from heaven and thrown to the devil.

Sophie found her mom and dad waiting in her room. Their faces said it all. They must have used the time during the fire alarm to talk about her.

"So, what did the doctor say?" Sophie asked.

Mom looked at Beatrice, who quickly left the room. Sophie's mom avoided looking at her as she spoke.

"You know doctors. Numbers and charts. The results are inconclusive. It's too soon for him to say."

Sophie knew better. In fact, she probably knew as much about her medication levels, blood cell counts, and stem cell transplants as the doctors. It hadn't worked, and Sophie had accepted that. She was no longer worried about herself. She was worried about Mom. Each failed treatment brought her mom closer to her breaking point. Dad was as stoic as ever, but Sophie knew he, too, was suffering.

They both needed time out of the hospital. Time where they could face up to reality and cry as much as they wanted without having to worry about putting up a brave front.

"Mom?"

"Yes, sweetie?"

"The fire drill wore me out. I need some rest. Why don't you and Dad go home early and get a good night's sleep? You can come back in the early afternoon and help me pack. That is, if you are still planning on checking me out tomorrow?"

"Of course, you are checking out. You know I hate the fact you have to stay in any hospitals even for a few days after a treatment, but now you're stable, and we have the..."

Mom's voice died, and she closed her eyes tightly. Dad moved to hold her hand. Sophie glanced away, giving her mom a few seconds to collect herself.

Her mom cleared her throat. "You'll feel better at home. Everything will be better when you get home."

Sophie knew her mother was trying to convince herself rather than Sophie. Sophie offered a bright smile and said, "Home would be good."

"Oh," Sophie's mom said, straightening. "What if you need us tonight?"

Relief washed through Sophie. It was better to see Mom's take-no-prisoners attitude than her watery smile. Sophie lifted the attention button attached to her bed. "I have Beatrice, Mom. She'll take care of me."

Dad got up and placed his hand on Mom's shoulder. "Come on, dear. Sophie's right. We need a good night's sleep, or we'll be of no use to her when she needs us."

"But..." Mom's voice cracked just a bit as she tried to stand.

Dad helped Mom get up and gently eased her out of the door with a grin toward Sophie. Dad was good like that. He was just as broken up inside as Mom, but he understood what Sophie needed. She loved that about him.

When they had gone, Sophie was unable to sit still, so she slid out of bed, careful of her IV tubes. At the window, she looked at the Mississippi River. Night had fallen, and the river spread out in front of her, dark except for the reflections of lights along the bank. A Carnival Cruise ship, adorned like a Christmas tree and filled with happy tourists setting out on an adventure, glided past. The Mississippi was once an artery for explorers and adventurers. Now, the waterway was an artery for trade and pleasure, and it highlighted many of the things Sophie would never be able to do.

Her short life had been a testament to her illness and the things she couldn't do. She couldn't go out to play at recess with the other kids because she was too frail and might hurt herself. Then, she couldn't attend school regularly due to treatments which were long and exhausting. Eventually, she was pulled out of school completely, distancing her from the few friends she had made. She spent long days alone learning from a computer while her mom searched for the next treatment, each time promising the next treatment would work.

This was the last treatment, highly experimental, and only available because Sophie was at an advanced stage. Sophie closed her eyes. She didn't want to die. Death terrified her, but she resigned herself to it because it would bring an end to her suffering. Though her pain had lessened since yesterday, Sophie was sure that was only temporary. Cancer was not a pleasant way to die.

She thought of Constance. Was she really a ghost? It didn't seem possible now. When she died would she become a ghost like Constance? Or would her soul just drift away?

A head popped through the wall next to Sophie. She stifled a scream once she realized it was Constance.

Constance smiled. "Hello, Miss Sophie. Have your parents gone?"

"Yes. Mom didn't want to go, but Dad convinced her it was for the best."

"What's wrong?"

"My treatment failed. They're not dealing well with the news."

"Oh, Sophie," Constance said, eyes bright with tears. "I'm so sorry."

Sophie shrugged her shoulders and walked back to her bed. "Don't be sorry for me. I should be sorry for you. Tell me more about this *gris-gris* and how I can help."

Constance stood by the end of Sophie's bed. "I shouldn't have asked you. You have your own troubles."

Sophie waved away her concern. "Meeting you has been the most exciting thing to happen to me. And since I don't have much longer to live, you should tell me everything."

"It's not a happy story," said Constance as she sat on a chair near the bed. "Are you sure you want to hear it?"

Sophie nodded. She needed to hear it.

"Marie Laveau is a powerful voodoo witch."

"Marie Laveau? If I recall my New Orleans history and legends right, didn't she die a long time ago?"

"She did." Constance nodded. "In 1881. She had a daughter, also named Marie Laveau, who also had a daughter called Marie Laveau, and so on until the Marie Laveau in this hospital, my current mistress."

"Mistress? Is this because of the charm?"

"My spirit is bound to the charm Marie wears around her neck. It has been passed from the first Marie Laveau, who cursed me and bound my soul, down to the present witch. They have prevented me from passing over to the afterlife. I've been like a slave to the Laveau family for a long time. When this Marie Laveau dies, I will serve her evil daughter."

Constance took a deep breath, seeming to gather herself. Sophie waited, fascinated with the story.

"I've got a man, or I had one back when I was alive. He worked on a Mississippi riverboat. He stole my breath away the first moment I saw his warm eyes. We were in love. Not a temporary love. Our love is eternal." Constance smiled, becoming lost in her memories.

Sophie tried to imagine a love like that. She couldn't. Wanting some sort of connection, Sophie tried to put her hand on Constance's knee, but it passed right through and touched the chair. She waved her hand up and down through Constance's leg.

This cheered Constance a little. "You is funny, Sophie."

"How can you sit on the chair and yet, my hand passes right through you?"

"I don't know. But I do know that I can do things like set off fire alarms, but the effort makes me tired."

Sophie laughed. "So, that was you who set off the alarm."

"Yes, miss. That was me." Constance's eyes twinkled with mischief. "I can't explain it, but you'll find these things out for yourself when you die. Oh... I'm so sorry."

"Don't worry about it. We all start dying from the day we're born. Everybody dies. Even the great Marie Laveau."

"You are wise, Sophie, for one so young."

"You were telling me about your man."

Constance beamed as if remembering him. "He's so pretty, and he's waiting for me. I see him once a year when the witch goes to Haiti for some festival or something. She don't want me coming because there are some powerful priests there and the witch is worried one of them will take me from her."

"What's his name?"

"Daniel, after the lions' den Daniel."

"That's a good name."

"He's a good man, too. Kind and brave, same as the Daniel who was thrown into the lions' den."

"I like him already," said Sophie. "Tell me more about this charm."

"I just thought. Oh, Sophie." Constance stood up with both arms raised. "The Lord might have answered your prayers."

"Calm down, Constance. Sit down and tell me about it."

"It's the charm. I don't know why I didn't think of this before. The charm. It's not an ordinary charm. It can purify your body and soul. The witch used it for evil, but I think it might cure your illness. I ain't positive. But the charm is powerful voodoo. If we can get it, we might be able to free me and cure you."

Was that possible? Sophie didn't believe it. She wanted to, but a voodoo charm curing cancer? No way. Yet, she had seen a ghost walk through walls and Constance had set off a fire alarm. It seemed that at the New Orleans Specialty Hospital of Stem Transplants, anything might be possible.

Sophie had been through too many treatments to get excited. She had a lot of her dad in her. And what would her God-fearing mom make of this voodoo cure? It must be the only thing they hadn't tried. Sophie didn't dare suggest something like that to her. She'd be desperate enough to haul her daughter to every voodoo practitioner in the Mississippi Delta if there was a chance it would cure her and if she found out about Haiti... Sophie didn't want to go to Haiti.

"Why doesn't the witch use the charm to cure her cancer? It doesn't make sense."

"She tried, but the charm didn't work for her. I heard her try it. I know the chant. I can say the chant for you. I think it didn't work because she is evil, pure evil. But you is good, Sophie."

Sophie wasn't so sure about that, although maybe she was compared to a voodoo witch.

"So. What's the plan?"

"The witch won't ever take that charm from around her neck except for tomorrow when she goes to surgery. The doctor insisted she remove it. She plans to leave it with the snake."

"The rubber snake that isn't really rubber and is poisonous?" Nothing about the witch made sense, and a normal person would run screaming from the room. But Sophie had never been normal, so she might as well try to wrap her brain around the craziness.

"It only looks rubber. Otherwise, they wouldn't let it in the hospital. The doctors and nurses think she's mad. She thinks they're stupid. It's a real snake, and she controls it. Somehow you have got to get the charm from the snake while the witch is in surgery."

"Will you be in surgery?" asked Sophie.

"No. That's one of the reasons for the snake. It guards the charm against me and others."

"Between the two of us, we might be able to get it from the snake. Can you pick up the charm?"

"Only for a few seconds. It takes all my concentration and energy to touch physical objects."

"Can the snake see you or hurt you?"

"It can't see me, but it can sense me. Marie's charmed it against me, and its touch paralyzes me. You're the one in real danger. Its bite will kill you."

"It has to catch me first," said Sophie. "I'll go in the room pretending to steal the charm, and while it's occupied with me, you can steal the charm."

"Sophie. That's too dangerous. It'll kill you."

"One," Sophie ticked the point off a finger, "I'm dying anyway. Two, I can use this if needed. I've seen my dad do it." Sophie pointed at her IV stand. Its pole was a long piece of metal bent at a right angle at the top, forming an arm with a hook where the IV bag hung from. It looked a bit like a snake hook.

"Sophie, this ain't no game. You can't be waving around your IV pole."

"That's only if it's necessary to fend off the snake. It will be fine. We can do this."

"What if your parents are here?"

"I'll send them out to get me something. Dad is always willing to sneak me in a treat the doctors don't want me to eat. Mom pretends she doesn't know about our game."

"I'm still not sure of this, Sophie."

"It's settled. We're doing it. I'm checking out tomorrow afternoon. It has to be done tomorrow morning. Come through the wall in the morning when the witch has left for surgery. If my parents are here, they can't see you anyway. I'll send them out and come next door."

"I don't know, Sophie. I don't think it will work."

"Constance, it will work. Now go before the wicked witch of New Orleans wakes up."

With a wave goodbye, Constance disappeared into the wall.

Was the solution as simple as stealing a charm? It seemed too easy. Take the charm, free Constance, and then, Constance would say the chant. The idea that she might be free from her illness was unbelievable. The doctors wouldn't believe it. Mom wouldn't believe it. But tests would prove it.

If it worked.

No way was Sophie going to tell her mom about the ghost and the voodoo witch. Mom would never believe that. But she'd believe that the preliminary tests were wrong and that this treatment really had cured her. Or maybe it would be a miracle. Mom wanted to believe in miracles. She had prayed long enough for one.

That was it. She'd give her mom a miracle. The thought warmed Sophie as she settled into her bed to sleep.

"SOPHIE, WAKE UP."

Sophie sat up in bed and reached for the light.

Constance paced the room, wringing her hands.

"What's going on?" Sophie asked, rubbing her eyes.

"Marie just had one of her fits, and the doctor canceled the operation for tomorrow. He said he'd reschedule it for a couple of days from now."

"Where's the witch now?"

"She's sleeping. The doctor gave her something to calm her nerves after the fit and help her sleep, but I should get back. She could wake up."

"Then, you should get back. But I'm going home tomorrow, Constance. I won't be able to help you if that surgery is postponed."

"It's enough that you wanted to help, Miss Sophie. That's more than anyone else has done."

"None of that 'miss' stuff. We're friends, remember?" Sophie had an idea. "This hospital is supposed to be full of ghosts. Maybe one of them can help you."

"You've seen them. I've been watching you wandering around at night. They are all wealthy plantation owners in their fine clothes."

"Those people are ghosts?"

"Yes. And they won't talk to the likes of me. I ain't got many friends."

"I'm your friend, Constance."

Constance forced a smile. "I know, Sophie. I know." The woman then lowered her head and disappeared into the wall.

The sight of her new friend's depression struck a devastating blow to Sophie's soul. She didn't have any good friends before she met Constance. She had wanted to help. To do something meaningful and lasting. Freeing a trapped ghost would have given her an accomplishment to be truly proud of in her short and limited life.

Sophie tried, but she couldn't sleep. She kept thinking about poor Constance and how she was probably next door, crying silently while that voodoo witch slept.

OMG! The wicked witch is asleep.

All she had to do was get the charm and open it to free Constance. She could tiptoe into the room and snatch the charm from the witch's neck. Marie Laveau might wake up, and the snake might get her, but she could save Constance.

Sophie jumped out of bed and grabbed her IV pole. She put her hat on and could almost hear the infamous Indiana Jones theme song.

She pulled the IV stand to the door. Just as she got there, one of the wheels squeaked. It hadn't been making any noise before, but now, it seemed loud enough to wake the dead. Sophie rolled her eyes. Nothing in her life was ever easy. She opened the door.

Sophie peeked around the corner. The hallway was empty.

The hospital was a three-story building with surgery on the bottom floor and five patient rooms on each of the top two floors. A nurse's station sat at the far end, by the elevator. Sophie could see the nurse's station. Surprisingly, the nurse was absent. At least, something was going her way. Sophie padded down the hallway and around the corner to the witch's room.

Just as she rounded the corner, the wheel on her IV stand stopped squeaking. Sophie thanked whoever was looking out for her as she halted in front of the ornate oak door. This was the moment, and everything was going to go smoothly. No nurse. No more squeaky wheel.

Sophie knew exactly what she planned to do. Open the door. Edge her way along the wall to the head of the bed. Grab the charm and open it. If she was quick, she might be able to do all that before the snake or the witch awoke to stop her.

The sound of Beatrice's no-nonsense, white sneakers echoed through the hallway. Sophie froze. She couldn't go back to her room without her nurse seeing her and didn't have time to duck into the witch's room without making any noise.

Sophie's eyes darted back and forth to the corner where Beatrice was coming from to the oak door. Her gaze fell upon just the thing that might save her. Across the hall was an empty alcove with a half-open sliding barn door. It would be the perfect place to hide for a few moments. Sophie pulled her IV stand into the alcove and pressed herself against the wall in the shadow.

Beatrice's sure footsteps moved closer and then stopped in front of the alcove. Sophie held her breath.

Please, please don't look in here.

"Funny, thought I heard something," said the nurse, looking around.

She turned and went back around the corner, presumably back to her station. As soon as the nurse had gone, Sophie left the alcove and approached the oak door again.

This is it. No turning away this time.

A skittering noise, like something with several legs, sounded from behind her. The skin on the back of her neck tingled. Slowly, Sophie turned her head to look at the hallway. A hairy, black spider, the size of a sheepdog, crouched inside of the alcove she had just occupied. Its shiny pincher-like fangs opened and closed, and multiple pairs of glistening, hungry eyes gazed at her.

Sophie bit back a scream, clutching at her IV pole until her fingers turned white. The stand's wheel gave several high-pitched squeaks as Sophie's arm quaked. The spider's fangs opened wide, and it reared up on its back legs. Sophie felt the bile in her stomach rise. She was going to die by spider bite in the hallway of a haunted hospital. Tremors racked Sophie's body. The frequency and pitch of the stand's wheel reached a soft, yet ear-shattering, screech. The spider feinted a lunge at Sophie and then jumped back into the darkness of the alcove, disappearing from sight.

Sophie waited, heart pounding, but she heard nothing. No more noises in the darkness. No rustling of eight giant legs. Sophie rubbed her hand along her collarbone, trying to soothe her frayed nerves and come to terms with what had just happened. Now, logically, the space hadn't been that large. The massive arachnid could have barely fit in there. But now, it was gone as mysteriously as it had appeared.

Sophie turned back to Marie's door. After that scare, the witch and her curses seemed tame. Gathering her courage, she put her hand on the handle and eased the door open. A soft creak filled Sophie's ears. Though the sound hadn't been loud, it sounded like a clap of thunder to her. Sophie's heart pounded, and her adrenalin spiked, making her feel light-headed.

Please, God or anyone listening. Help me do this. Help me make my life mean something.

Sophie sucked in air, calmed herself, and looked into the room. A wedge of light streamed in through the open door, offering a view of the end of Marie Laveau's bed. Sophie couldn't see the witch or Constance, so she waited, listening. A low, rasping breathing came from the bed. The witch was sleeping, but where was Constance?

It didn't matter. Sophie had a plan. She sidestepped with her back to the wall, edging carefully toward the head of the bed. Her eyes had adjusted to the dark, allowing her to see the shadow form of the witch. Two steps from the bed, mattress springs groaned as Marie Laveau shifted. Sophie nearly jumped out of her skin. But the witch didn't wake. She resettled herself and began snoring.

Fear churned in Sophie's stomach as she waited until Marie returned to breathing evenly and calmly. She had to get the charm and now. Marie could wake up at any moment, Beatrice could decide to peek in on her charges, or that spider could come back. Besides, Sophie wasn't feeling well. Either all the activity, or the fear, had Sophie feeling weak and nauseated.

Sophie drew another deep breath. She could see the large oval-shaped charm around the neck of the sleeping witch. A few seconds. She could find the courage to last that long.

Sophie edged closer, seeing the even rise and fall of Marie's chest. Carefully, she reached out until her hand was inches from the charm. The wheel on her IV stand chose that moment to squeak. Sophie paused, fingers shaking.

Stupid wheel. Save me from a spider, but throw me to the witch.

But the noise hadn't awakened the witch.

A hiss of air escaped Sophie's lips, and she decided to go for it. She touched the chain and tried to move it around the witch's neck to get to the clasp. The woman stopped snoring. The silence unnerved Sophie, but she continued until she could see the clasp. The witch grunted and started snoring again.

With unsteady fingers, she tugged on the chain and leaned in to undo the clasp. The clasp was old and awkward, but after three tries, she opened it. Sophie closed her eyes and willed her frantic beating heart to calm. There. The hard part was done. All she had to do was take the charm and open it.

Sophie reached out, wrapping her fingers around the charm, but the instant she lifted the charm from the witch's neck, Marie's eyes snapped open. Her head turned to stare straight at Sophie. Sophie gazed into her eyes and saw raw, primal power and pure evil. The witch had no soul.

———

SOPHIE HELD the charm in her hand. All she had to do was snatch it away and run. Her hand moved, but the older woman was lightning-fast, and Sophie felt a vice-like grip grab her hand. She cried out as the woman's icy-cold fingers dug into her wrist. Sophie tried to get away but found the old woman to be surprisingly strong.

Terrified and desperate, Sophie put everything she had into pulling her arm away. Her illness had weakened her, but adrenalin coursed through her, and even though the witch's nails raked her skin, she was able to wrench the charm away.

"Sophie. What you doing?"

Sophie whirled around toward Constance's voice.

"I've got the charm." Sophie held it up, showing Constance. "I just need to open it."

"No!" the witch screamed. "No. Give that back to me."

Sophie felt the words as much as she heard them. There was power in that voice, power in those words, compelling her to return the charm to the witch. Sophie wouldn't do it, couldn't do it. This was Constance's freedom at risk, and maybe hers.

"No," Sophie said, turning to face the witch and trying to put as much steel into her voice as she could.

The compulsion to obey dissipated, and Sophie took the opportunity to flee the room.

Gasping for air after her race to her room, Sophie focused on opening the charm and removing the hair. Her fingers fumbled with the charm's latch. It took her two tries, but she pulled Constance's hair free. An instant later, Constance came through the wall, startling her.

"You did it, Sophie. Bless you, child. You did it." Constance put her arms around Sophie.

Sophie couldn't feel the hug, but she sensed a warmth enclosing her. It lightened her heart to know that her friend could move on now and be with her love.

Constance withdrew. "Now you. Where's the charm?"

"You scared me, and I dropped it." Sophie looked around her feet for the charm. "There. Near my bed."

A long black snake slithered over her foot, and Sophie screamed. She scrambled back, moving to grab her IV pole and defend herself.

"It's going for the charm, Sophie."

Lightning-quick, the snake snapped up the charm. Sophie brandished her IV pole, shaking it at the snake. It hissed at her as best as it could with the charm wedged in its mouth.

"Stop!"

The snake slithered back, moving closer to the door. Sophie took off after it.

"No, Sophie. Don't."

Sophie ignored Constance and smashed the pole down at the snake. She'd put too much force into her blow, and the pole went wide, missing her target. Sophie lost her balance and fell forward. The snake took the opportunity to slither out the door.

"Are you okay, Miss Sophie?"

Sophie lay dazed on the floor, trying to gather herself. Pain shot through her body. It flashed from her banged knees straight to her head. She could barely think past the pain, but every instinct screamed at her to get up and get that charm.

Sophie pushed to her feet, swaying slightly while she stared dumbly at her IV pole at her feet. "I need to get the charm back."

"No, it's too dangerous. I'll get it. Marie has no hold on me anymore."

"I can't let you do that."

Sophie's head snapped to the doorway as she heard someone. Slouched over a crooked, wooden cane stood the voodoo witch Marie Laveau, dressed in a silky black top and flowing black skirt. She opened her palm, flashing the golden charm.

"Is this what you want, child?"

Sophie hated that woman more than she had ever thought it possible to hate anyone. How could there be so much evil in one person?

"You, old witch. Give it to me," Sophie said as she moved closer.

A gurgling laugh came from the witch's throat. She held up the charm.

"Come and get it, child."

"Fine, I will."

"No, Sophie," Constance shouted. "It's a trap."

Before Sophie could react, the snake appeared behind Marie's voluminous skirt. Its long serpentine body was poised like a spring, and it lunged at Sophie's bare foot. Sharp, stinging pain lanced through Sophie. Her muscles seized, and she dropped to the floor.

Constance's futile cries for someone to help Sophie were

drowned out by the old witch's cackles of laughter. "Now, you're mine."

Razor blades of agony tore through Sophie's body. She always knew she'd die in pain, but this wasn't how she'd pictured it. She rolled to her side, spotting something famil-iar. With her last bit of strength, Sophie reached out and wrapped her fingers around the brim of her hat.

I'm ready for the greatest adventure, Daddy.

SOPHIE AND CONSTANCE stood on the hill overlooking the cemetery watching the funeral—Sophie's funeral. Her mom and dad stood amongst the mourners, Mom crying without reservation, Dad remaining stoic and holding on to his weeping wife.

Sophie wanted to go down there and have a group hug like they had in the hospital, but she couldn't. There was a limit to how far she was able to travel whilst her mistress, the voodoo witch, slept and the brow of the hill was her limit.

"Sophie, I'm so sorry. I never wanted this to happen to you."

"Don't apologize. I was going to die soon anyway. I've been dying since I was born." Sophie held her friend's hand.

"It's not the dying, Sophie. I've made a decision. I'm going to go see the witch and ask her to take me back instead of you."

Sophie let go of Constance's hand and turned to face her. "Don't you dare. I got myself into this, and I'll get myself out of it."

"But Sophie – "

"Constance. Think of Daniel. You have a chance for

happiness now. Anyway. If you try, the witch will probably double-cross you, and we'll both be bound to her."

"You is right. She's an evil woman."

Sophie took both Constance's hands. "I can handle her."

She saw some of the giant spiders from the hospital on the hill beside her; they'd followed her around since she'd become a ghost. She knew Constance was unable to see them, so she never mentioned them to her.

Sophie squeezed Constance's fingers and smiled. "Don't worry. She's going to be sorry she ever made a slave of me." Sophie paused. "I can't believe she got those bits of my skin from under her fingernails to make the charm – the *gris-gris*."

Constance smiled, but it was forced. "My Daniel and I will do everything in our power to help you."

Sophie felt the line of power tug on her. "I have to go. The old witch calls."

Sophie put on her hat, covering her long hair, which had returned since her death. She smiled once more at Constance.

"The witch doesn't like the hat."

A moment later, an unseen force drew Sophie away from the funeral and back to her mistress, the voodoo witch, Marie Laveau.

ABOUT THE AUTHORS

Christopher Wills

Christopher Wills is Soldier Sailor Teacher Trainer Storyteller. He writes YA fantasy in his Lulu Love Teenage Ghost series and military Sci-Fi based on his own experiences! He lives in the UK, loves rugby, running, folk and blues music, and plays the Ukulele and Harmonica badly. You can find Christopher at his website www.crwills.com on Twitter as Lulughost and on FB.

Ashley Lauren

Ashley Lauren's motto is Live Your Adventure! She tries to abide by that philosophy and live her life to the fullest every second. She's jumped out of planes, flown in the backseat of an F-15, gone to pilot training, been an engineer in the Air Force, studied satellites and radars, lived all over the US and in England, and survived the greatest adventure of all, motherhood. Other than her wonderful husband and four beautiful daughters, the highlight of her life was hanging out of the back of a Black Hawk helicopter flying 100ft over the treetops at night.

Come step out of your world and into Ashley's to see what adventures she has waiting for you.

Become a VIP reader at www.ashleylaurenbooks.wixsite.com/yaparanormal

THE CASKET GIRLS

BY ZACH BOHANNON and J. Thorn

ALEX PEERED through the smudged glass face of the CD jukebox against the wall. It had been years since the old machine had spun discs by The Clash, the Sex Pistols, and dozens of other seminal gothic and punk rock classics. Alex preferred Siouxsie over Blondie, but any loud, fast music would be better than the violent screams coming from the streets of the French Quarter. The votives she'd stolen from the Voodoo Museum sat on the edge of the bar, the short flames burning straight and true in the sealed room.

She wore black leather pants and a black t-shirt, her auburn hair with blonde streaks flaring out from her temples. At twenty-five, Alex could get by on three hours of sleep and a burrito for breakfast while still being fit enough to kick the ass of men twice her size.

The Jimani Bar and Lounge stank of stale beer and clove cigarettes, even though nobody had lit up inside the dive bar for years, thanks to the New Orleans' smoking ban. With the grid down and the crazies in the Quarter acting more insane than usual, the Casket Girls had padlocked the doors in the hopes of keeping the crowds out—and themselves in.

Alex climbed the rickety stairs and sat in the corner of the room with her knees pulled up to her chin. The Casket Girls had retreated to the top floor of the building as the floodwaters continued to rise. Most of the girls sat quietly in small groups or played cards at a rickety table propped against the far wall. Evelyn had said they would need to relocate their headquarters and archives eventually, but they'd stay at The Jimani for as long as possible.

"Where in the hell are they?" Saw asked, running her hand along the side of her shaven head, an unlit stub of a cigarette pinched between her index and middle finger. "They've been gone since early this afternoon."

Alex glanced at Evelyn. "They'll be back." She wasn't sure even *she* believed the words coming from her mouth.

"How do you know?" Saw lit her cigarette stub and winced from the first, bitter drag. The woman's tattoos spread over a thin but muscular build, her almond-shaped eyes like snares beneath a platinum-blond mohawk.

"This isn't the first time we've sent out Scout and her crew."

"I'm not so sure," Saw said. "I mean, they were supposed to—"

"They'll *be* back," Alex said, assassinating Saw's sentence before she could finish it.

Saw scoffed, taking one last hit before snuffing out her cigarette in an empty can of Pabst Blue Ribbon. "Whatever you say." She stood up.

"Where are you going?" Zoe asked.

Zoe's long braids framed a face with a sneer that could have cut steel. She grew up in the heart of the African-

American community of New Orleans, her ancestors having escaped the plantations after the Civil War.

"To see what the others are up to."

Saw walked to the other end of the room where several other Casket Girls sat around the table littered with empty cans of PBR and souvenir playing cards with iconic photographs of New Orleans' landmarks on the back—no doubt lifted from a tourist trap on Bourbon Street.

Zoe waited until Saw sat down and was dealt in before walking over and patting Alex on the knee.

"She's just nervous. We all are. We all want them to return safely."

"And they will. This is what *she's* trained us for."

They both looked over to the older, slender woman standing by the window. Evelyn Winter had pulled her hair back into a single, braided ponytail with wisps of gray tucked behind her ears. Her deep, brown eyes darted around the room, pausing to make momentary eye contact with Alex and Zoe. Evelyn wore black jeans with holes in the knees and a brown leather jacket that was either two sizes too large or had belonged to a man. She turned back to the window and stared down onto Chartres Street, her arms crossed with one hand on her chin.

"What do you see?" Alex asked although she knew the woman would reply only when she had a satisfactory answer.

She had been a teenager when Evelyn had spared her from a life on the streets. Alex had fled from an abusive father who used various addictions to fill the holes left by the death of his wife, Alex's mother, when the girl was only twelve years old. Evelyn had become a mother to Alex. In fact, she had become the mother of *all* the Casket Girls.

The woman turned around. The poker game stopped, and a cold draft of silence filled the room.

Alex looked up again at Evelyn who had been quiet for hours.

"I know you're worried about Scout, Jen, Razor, Klara, and Flash, but I can assure you that they are serving the greater good. In the meantime, we must stay alert."

She scanned the room. Alex had been mentored by Evelyn for several years and had unofficially risen to her second-in-command.

"Alex."

The sound of her name broke Alex out of her daze. She turned her attention to the front of the room and saw not only her sisters looking at her but her mentor staring at her as well.

"Yes?"

Evelyn glided, her feet making soft thumps on the warped, oak floor. The others resumed their conversations, and Alex stood up. She smiled at Zoe before joining Evelyn at the far side of the room where the two had some privacy. Alex saw through the older woman's shallow smile, the wrinkles on her forehead deepening.

"What's wrong?"

Evelyn stood, facing away from Alex and staring at the wall as if it held a priceless painting.

"The darkness has returned, and the others are not back."

Alex sighed. "You have trained us well. They can handle themselves out there. And if they need help, we'll go out there and help them."

"Good." Evelyn finally turned her eyes to Alex. "You are strong, and I need you to make sure you can hold the others together. Your sisters are scared. You *must* be there for them."

"I will, but you are here, too... I don't understand?"

Evelyn turned back to the wall and placed her hand on her forehead. Alex had spent enough time with her to know when the woman was tapping into her mental channels. Papa Midnight had taught Evelyn how to use the Sight, and in turn, Evelyn had started teaching it to Alex.

Someone downstairs slammed the brass door knocker. Alex spun around and faced the steps leading down to The Jimani.

"They're back." Steph rushed past Alex and stopped at the top of the steps, the banging from downstairs becoming more rapid.

Alex followed Steph down the stairs and stood in front of the jukebox next to Zoe and Saw, who'd also raced down to greet Scout and her girls as they returned.

Steph ran along the bar and leaped over an overturned stool, unlatching the four locks and pulling on the heavy, wooden door. The entrance sat at the top of three steps which was how high the water had risen. It would only be a few hours before the floodwaters would start oozing into the bar.

A girl stumbled inside and dropped down on all fours. Her matted hair stuck to her face and grime covered her arms from wrist to shoulder beneath a ragged black t-shirt. Steph kneeled next to her and helped the girl into a chair.

"My God, Scout," Steph said. "What happened? Where are the others?"

Scout—whose real name was Brianna—was the leader of the Casket Girls' lookout crew. At only nineteen, she was the youngest of the Casket Girls holed up in The Jimani, and her small frame and uncanny sense of smell made her perfect for the role.

She mumbled something under her breath.

"What?" Steph asked, leaning her ear toward Scout's mouth.

"Shut the goddamn door!"

The words came sharp and fast, blowing Steph back and onto her ass. Alex gasped. Lily and Buzz hurried to the door, slamming it shut and sliding the stainless-steel deadbolts into place.

With the screams and sounds of chaos now muted, Scout's heavy breathing was the only sound in the tiny, cramped dive bar.

Tears ran down her face, cutting stark, white lines through the smeared blood on her cheeks. A bruise beneath her left eye had swollen it shut.

"Jesus," Zoe said. "What happened?"

Saw headed for the door. "I'm gonna beat the shit out of whoever did this to you."

"No!"

Everyone turned to see Evelyn standing in the middle of the room. Saw stopped and leaned against the bar, her arm resting on a dry tap.

Evelyn walked toward Scout. The young woman climbed to her feet as her mentor approached. Scout slouched, and she stared up at Evelyn while blood dripped off her fingertips.

"It's worse than we thought," Scout said, shaking her head. "It's all about to end."

ALEX STARED AIMLESSLY as Scout's words disintegrated into a

ragged cough.

Could she be talking about...

"Help me get her upstairs and on the bed," Steph said.

Zoe, Steph, and Alex picked up Scout and lifted her to her feet. The girl's shoulders collapsed, and Alex felt the warm, sticky drip of blood on her hand.

They guided Scout up the steps to the second floor which was still dry... for now.

A single bed had been pushed into the corner of the room. Alex had told the girls it belonged to Evelyn, and yet every morning, the older woman woke up on the floor, surrounded by her girls—the bed untouched.

Saw ran over to help lower Scout onto it, placing her on her back.

"Move your asses and get us some towels!" Saw said.

Several of the Casket Girls shuffled around the room, rifling through cabinets and the shelves beneath them, looking for anything that resembled linens.

Alex looked into Scout's bloodshot eyes. She ran her hand through the girl's knotted hair and planted a single kiss on her forehead. A hand landed on Alex's shoulder, and she could smell Zoe's sweet, tart breath—the girl loved her cherry candies.

"Let's give her some space," Zoe said. "She'll talk when she's ready."

"We need to talk now." Scout tried to sit up, but Alex eased her back down.

"There will be time."

"No, that's what you don't understand. There *isn't* time."

"At least let us clean you up while you explain."

Scout shook her head, trying to sit up again. "We don't have time for this. We have to—"

"Alex is right."

Alex turned toward the center of the room where Evelyn stood with her arms folded across her chest. The girls faced Evelyn, all of them silent.

"We must tend to your wounds—stop that bleeding from that gash in your shoulder. I will not lose any more of my girls tonight."

Evelyn had known about Scout's injury even before the girl had removed her coat. But that flicker of Sight was not what sent a shiver up Alex's spine. Although nobody in the room had addressed it yet, the girls knew the bitter truth—Scout had left The Jimani with her team and had come back alone.

Alex had tried to ignore the obvious. She had busied herself with Scout, doting on her like a feeble child to take her mind off the reality Evelyn had probably seen while she was staring onto Chartres Street from the upstairs window.

A low groan broke the silence as Zoe and Steph tended to Scout's injuries, using whatever dirty rags they could find to apply pressure to the wounds that continued to ooze blood.

"I'm sorry," Zoe said. "We're almost done."

Scout coughed and winced, her hand going up to her injured shoulder. The girls had wiped the blood from her face and now fresh tears of pain ran in ragged lines down her cheek. Scout pulled herself up and leaned against the headboard, closing her eyes and breathing heavily.

Evelyn sat on the edge of the bed, took Scout's hand in hers, and leaned in with a whisper.

"Now, tell us what happened."

Scout opened her eyes and stared at Evelyn. The woman placed a delicate phrase into the girl's ear, and Scout nodded as she exhaled.

"We wanted to check the Quarter again. I know you'd

advised us against that, and I'm sorry. But I had one of those feelings I get. Even Jen told me it was a stupid—"

"It's all right," Evelyn said. "You don't have to justify your intuition. Go on."

Scout licked her lips and nodded. "We finished at the corner of North Peters and Bienville. The sun was starting to go down. I knew we shoulda been back already but I... I felt something. And then, we heard people above that restaurant on the corner, Felipe's, crying out for help, so Klara pulled the boat up to the building. Both Jen and Flash said we should keep moving, but those people sounded like they needed help. I couldn't just leave them to die."

Scout lowered her head. She ran the back of her hand across her eyebrows and sniffled. When she looked up again, Alex could see fresh tears forming in the corners of her eyes. Saw reached into her pocket for her cigarettes, took one out, and placed it between Scout's lips. Saw then flipped open a Saints' Zippo and lit the cigarette for Scout.

"Thanks." Scout took the first drag and exhaled deeply, blowing a thick cloud of smoke into the air.

"No problem. Whenever you're ready..."

Scout took another drag and then continued.

"We should have never gone in there. They must have seen us coming from a long ways out and started yelling. When we got inside, there was a screaming woman. I asked if she was all right, and before I knew it, there were four gangsters in the room pointing rifles at us. Flash stepped forward to say something, and one of the men shot her in the chest before she even had a chance to speak."

Gasps came from every corner of the room. Alex covered her mouth and clenched her eyes shut, trying to remember the last thing she had said to Flash—to all of the girls who had not returned.

"They would have killed Razor, too, but I held her back. Then the man who killed Flash screamed at us, saying that we were his 'property' now. He led us upstairs at gunpoint. When we came out of the stairwell, I looked past him into a room and saw a group of girls tied up. He said to me, 'That's why I killed the ugly one. The rest of you are premium product.' At that point, I was gripping Razor's arm so tightly that my nails were digging into her skin. The man was about to take us into the room with the other girls when a horrific scream came from the room next door. I knew something wasn't right by the way the guy reacted. He told his men to go check it out, and he stayed back to make sure we didn't go anywhere.

"All we heard after that was shouting and gunshots. The building lit up with muzzle flashes. The place reeked of gunpowder. And although we couldn't see anything, we heard the high-pitched, shrill sounds after the guns stopped firing.

"Then the guttural growling came, and we knew what it was."

"Vamps," Alex mumbled. She felt everyone in the room turn to her.

Scout nodded.

"The men had taken our weapons and left them downstairs, so we couldn't fight. We had no choice but to run.

"There was a door in the ceiling that led to the roof. Since I was the smallest, Razor lifted me up onto her shoulders and told me to open it. Get out first.

"I got the hatch opened, climbed the short ladder, and pulled myself up onto the roof. And that's when I heard the screams again. This time, it wasn't from somewhere inside the building. It was from inside of the *room*.

"Razor looked up at me and yelled at me to run, and then a Vamp came out of nowhere and tackled her."

Alex closed her eyes, her Sight showing her glimpses of the scene Scout had witnessed.

Blood. Pain. Death.

"More came, and I was about to jump down to try and help them, but all I heard was, 'Run, Scout. Get help!'"

"And so you did."

The question posed as a statement came from Wall. At six-foot-two, Wall towered over the other Casket Girls. She wore long dreadlocks, her dark arms ripped with muscles.

"I didn't have a choice," Scout said. "There were so many of them. I—"

Wall said, "Of course you had a damn choice. We all have a fucking choice. And I would never *choose* to leave one of my sisters behind. Never."

"You weren't there, Wall," Zoe said. "You can't judge her."

"Don't tell me what I can and can't do, you light-skinned bitch."

"Hey, don't you talk to her like that," Saw said, moving between Zoe and Wall.

"Yeah? What you gonna do about it with that nappy-ass shaved head and shit?"

Saw gritted her teeth and took another step forward, but three girls grabbed her by the arms, including Alex. It took four other Casket Girls to hold back Wall. They lobbed insults like grenades as the others in the room shouted, trying to take sides.

"Silence!"

Alex turned to see Evelyn's red face, her eyes glistening and scanning the room.

"We cannot turn on each other. I won't have it!"

Before anyone could respond, a piercing screech came

from the street below. Scout's eyes went wide, and she jumped out of bed.

"They're here."

The girls stared at each other. For most of these women, their study with Evelyn had been theoretical. Sure, they had seen flashes of the creatures delivered via the older woman's Sight, but that wasn't the same as standing face-to-face with the Vamps now overrunning the streets of New Orleans.

"Grab your weapons and head for the roof," Evelyn said. "We have a better chance of fighting them off if we get the high ground."

Alex ran to the corner of the second-floor room and grabbed her satchel. She opened it and glanced at the nearly dozen stakes she'd made before the grid had gone dark. The Casket Girls had known they would come—that this day was inevitable. Alex had long been prepared.

Zoe and Saw also grabbed their weapons. Zoe carried a bag like Alex's, filled with stakes and a dagger with a silver blade. Saw tossed her crossbow over a shoulder and picked up her weapon of choice—a baseball bat with silver nails embedded in it. She eyed the fat end of the bat before spinning it in her hand.

"You really going to take that thing up there?" Zoe asked. "Let's hope they're not already on the roof."

"Dorothy?" Saw looked at the bat and smiled. "Of course. If they are, she's gonna knock those fuckers right back into Oz."

Evelyn motioned to the girls. They followed her up the steps to the third floor where other Casket Girls had been grabbing their own personal arsenals, getting ready to fight. Evelyn stood beneath the hatch, ready to speak.

"This is what we have prepared for. Nothing stands between them and complete annihilation of our world—but us. We are the ones with the knowledge to defeat them, and if you must sacrifice yourself for the greater good, then so be it."

The women tapped the sharp edges of their weapons against the floor, the wall, or their body armor. Alex looked around and saw both the fear and adrenaline on her sisters' faces.

Wall reached up and pulled on a stainless-steel ring, allowing the ladder to slide down the rails until the bottom step rested on the floor. Evelyn climbed up first. She opened the hatch, and the sounds of distant screams and gunfire filled the third-floor room. Alex looked at Zoe and then to Saw, both women grimacing but with a devilish smile underneath it. They nodded at her as several other Casket Girls went up the ladder behind Evelyn. Alex went next, Zoe and Saw the last two waiting to ascend to battle. Saw climbed halfway up, paused, and looked down at her two closest friends.

"Let's slay these fuckers."

───────

THE CASKET GIRLS stood in a circle on the roof. Alex took her spot in-between Zoe and Saw, gripping a stake in both hands. Heavy clouds blocked the moonlight and darkened the skies, dropping visibility to near nothing in a city without electricity. But the women had prepared for this. Evelyn had trained them while blindfolded, knowing they'd most likely have to fight the creatures in total darkness. Alex took a deep breath and focused her ears on the shrieks drawing ever closer to The Jimani.

"Be ready, and keep the circle tight," Evelyn said. "We mustn't allow them into the building."

Alex tried not to think about the wealth of information and research they'd gathered over the years. Sure, some of that had been digitized and stored on flash drives throughout the city, but what good would that do without electricity? And if the Vamps made it inside and realized what they'd found, they'd destroy the building along with the memory of many Casket Girls who had died to build the archives. She believed the creatures were being drawn to Evelyn—the double-edged sword of the Sight. The same power that could defeat them was also what attracted them. For now, the Casket Girls' archive would be safe. But for how long?

On top of the building across the street, Alex noticed three sets of orange, glowing eyes. She heard the muffled thumps as the creatures launched themselves through the air and landed on the brick façade of their building.

"They're coming," Zoe said.

The first high-pitched scream came from in front of Alex. The Vamp's head popped up from the edge of the building, its orange eyes glaring at them. It leaped up and landed two feet from Blaze. Blaze's blonde hair whipped around as she grunted, swinging her katana and decapitating the orange-eyed creature.

Another scream. A second creature climbed over the wall and onto the roof, running full speed at Alex. She raised her right hand and aimed a stake at its chest, but the creature doubled over and collapsed at her feet. Saw stepped on the Vamp's back and pulled the bat from the back of its head with a sickening squish. She then spit on the creature before looking up at Alex.

"We got this. Stay focused."

Alex nodded and reassumed her position in their circle.

These girls were not going to allow each other to die. She trusted them, and they trusted her.

Don't let them down the ladder, Alex.

She nodded in response to Evelyn's mental message.

Several more creatures roared on the roof of the building across the street. They leaped off the edge of the roof and flew, landing on the roof of The Jimani and within five feet of Alex.

"I've got the one on the left."

She allowed the creature to come closer, then she lunged forward and drove a stake into its heart.

To her right, Zoe groaned. Another one of the Vamps had grabbed her by the hair, but Zoe kicked it in the gut twice, and it let go. She then drove her stake into its heart, extinguishing the glow in its eyes.

More Vamps jumped across the chasm between the two buildings, raining down on the Casket Girls in a whirlwind of screams. The women held the circle as the pile of Vamp bodies grew before them.

"Hold position," Evelyn said. "They're about to send more."

Four more creatures dropped onto the roof in front of Alex. She heard whistles coming from her left, followed by the sound of bones cracking. One at a time, the Vamps cried out and fell backward over the edge of the roof, their bodies splashing in the floodwaters below.

Saw stood next to Alex, pulling arrows from her quiver.

"Dumb motherfuckers." Saw smirked as she loaded another bolt into the barrel.

A chorus of screams came from the west side of the building.

"Jesus," Steph said, her back to Alex and facing the other side of the roof.

Alex looked past Steph and saw dozens of the creatures gathering on the roof of an adjacent building. Their orange eyes appeared, glowing in the darkness with a wicked warning. By the time Saw shook Alex by the arm, at least two dozen Vamps had lined up on the other building's roof, ready to launch into the fight—double the number of Casket Girls holding the circle on the roof of The Jimani.

"They've alerted others of our presence," Scout said. "We can't beat them all."

"The fuck we can't," Saw said.

"Yeah, no one moves," Wall said.

"Do you want to die up here?" Scout asked. "We have to leave! We have to retreat and give up The Jimani."

Wall said, "The hell we—"

"Scout is right." Evelyn's commanding voice cut through the growing rumble of snarls coming from the roof of the adjacent building. "We've done our best, but we have to give up the archives to save ourselves. Everybody back down the ladder. Now!"

ALEX HELD the hatch open while the other women retreated down to the top level of The Jimani. She slammed the hatch shut as three more creatures landed on the roof. She grabbed the slide bolt and locked it, trying to catch her breath.

"We've got to get out of this building before they break through the hatch," Evelyn said, standing by the window. "Our lives are more important than the archive. Everyone into the boats."

The water had risen, but the ground was still two stories beneath them. Several of the girls swung their legs out onto the fire escape and scampered down as more screeching came from the roof.

Alex heard the sound of metal on metal as the Vamps tore through the hatch and entered the top floor of the building. She looked down and saw two small boats that would barely hold the ten or eleven Casket Girls that needed to use them to escape the attack. She ushered everyone through the window and down the fire escape until it was just her and Evelyn.

"Go," Evelyn said.

Alex jumped through the window, down the fire escape, and into the same boat with her two closest friends, Zoe and Saw.

The sound of breaking glass preceded billowing smoke coming from the windows on the third floor. The creatures above them screamed, and their macabre chorus sent a chill up Alex's spine.

"We've got to go now!" Zoe said, her face turned up to Evelyn who stood at the top of the fire escape, silhouetted against the gray haze.

Evelyn ran down the escape and leaped into the other boat. Saw didn't wait to take off. She gunned the outboard motor, pulling in front of the boat Evelyn and the others were in. Zoe, Alex, Wall, Scout, and Steph 'sat in the boat piloted by Saw.

"Don't get too far ahead of them," Steph said.

"They'll catch up," Saw said, giving the motor more gas.

"No!" Wall said. "We can't leave them behind."

"Saw is right," Alex said. "Evelyn wouldn't want us to wait. They'll catch up."

Before Wall or Steph could object, the sound of the second motorboat came from behind. Evelyn's boat had also escaped from The Jimani and was only a few yards away.

Alex smiled. But it quickly faded when she heard the cries of at least a half-dozen creatures. She looked up and saw three pass by their boat as they scaled across the vertical surface of the buildings. One even stared down with its orange eyes, but it didn't attack them. In fact, the Vamps seemed to be keeping pace with the other boat.

"What are they doing?" Wall asked.

"I don't know," Alex said. She watched the creatures gathering on the buildings and rooftops. And even though there were two boats full of Casket Girls, the Vamps seemed to be more interested in Evelyn's boat. Alex felt a flash of the Sight and screamed at Saw.

"Turn the boat around!"

"Why?" Scout asked.

Alex glared at Scout. "Turn the goddamn boat around, Saw!"

Without hesitating, Saw turned around and headed for Evelyn's boat.

"Holy shit," Scout said, Alex's revelation now hitting her like a bucket of ice water to the face. "They're after *Evelyn*."

Saw pulled alongside the other boat as one of the Vamps leaped from a nearby roof, landed in Evelyn's boat, and grabbing Blaze by the throat.

"Hurry!" Alex said.

The creature put both hands around Blaze's throat, and with a sharp crack, snapped her neck. Blaze went limp as the Vamp dropped her dead body into the water.

"No!" Saw said. She grabbed her bat and jumped into the other boat.

The fight turned into a blur as Alex maneuvered between the Sight and reality. She saw Casket Girls dying and orange eyes everywhere. A sudden thump in the middle of her back brought a flash of pain. Weightlessness. Then the sensation of slick, oily water followed by an explosion that lit the sky before the darkness swallowed it. Girls screamed, and Alex felt someone grab her shoulder. She had been pulled back onto the boat, soaking wet and shivering. Saw stood over her, screaming her name but Alex could only hear ringing in her head.

Zoe, Wall, Kris, Scout, Steph, and Evelyn appeared above her and Alex felt the craft shift. Saw had gunned the motor, pitching the front end of the boat into the air. The other boat was already on fire, the rest of the Casket Girls missing or dead.

More creatures screamed from above, but Saw was pulling away faster than they could run.

Evelyn sat at the front of the boat, her head buried in her bloody hands. She wasn't upset. Alex had never seen her cry. But she could see Evelyn shaking, and Alex felt her despair through the Sight.

Alex went to the woman and put an arm around her.

"Now what?" Saw asked.

SAW STEERED the boat deeper into the French Quarter, the sounds of the creatures fading behind them. Alex couldn't tell exactly where they were. It was too dark, and she hadn't been paying attention enough to keep her bearings. She'd been too busy worrying about Evelyn.

The leader of the Casket Girls hadn't spoken. The other girls had been silent as well.

In a matter of hours, all but seven of the Casket Girls had been wiped out. Evelyn had warned the girls that this was going to be a treacherous battle, but Alex had never expected anything this dire.

Saw brought the boat to a stop, looking around but apparently not seeing any threats.

"What are you doing?" Wall asked.

"What does it look like?" Saw said, her arms out. "I'm fucking stopping."

"No shit, but why? We need to keep moving."

"Who made you the boss?"

"That's not my point. We've got to put more distance between us and those things, you stupid bitch."

Saw sneered. "What the fuck did you—"

"Stop it!"

Evelyn erupted, standing up and almost falling out of the boat. She slapped Wall across the face and then did the same to Saw. The other women gasped.

Other than during their training, Alex had never seen Evelyn strike any of the girls. She'd always treated them like her own daughters. And in many ways, they were. And that's why Alex felt so much pain radiating through the Sight. Alex had lost her sisters, but for Evelyn, she'd lost her children.

"We have no hope of winning if we're fighting each other. Stop the bickering and let's take an inventory of who and what we have right now. We're going to need to—"

A long, shrill scream reverberated off the surrounding buildings.

They've found us.

"Get us out of here," Alex said.

Saw pulled away, speeding down the nearest side street.

Steph grabbed a military-grade flashlight from underneath her seat and aimed it at the front of the boat. "Shit."

The flashlight's beam hit a brick wall. A dumpster floated at the end of the alley, which was a dead end.

"Turn it around, Saw," Alex said.

As Saw steered them around, a set of orange eyes appeared on the roof of the building above the alley.

"Go!"

Saw gunned it but the motor coughed, sputtered, and then shut off. The other girls gasped and Saw hit the ignition button several times.

"Shit," Saw grabbed Steph's shoulder. "Shine that light down here so I can see what I'm doing."

The fuel gauge was in the red. Saw reached around and looked for an auxiliary tank switch, hoping whoever owned the boat was smart enough to install a marine fuel bladder.

The screams in the near distance seemed to get closer. Alex looked up to the roof to see that the creature above had disappeared.

Where did it go?

"Hurry the hell up," Wall said. "What are you doing?"

"Patience is a fucking virtue," Saw said, flipping the rocker that would switch the fuel line from the main tank to the reserve bladder.

A crash sounded near the right side of the boat, and all the girls looked toward it. Steph aimed the flashlight in the direction of the sound.

A single Vamp stood on a fire escape leading up to the roof of the building. The creature's orange eyes glowed, the malevolent forces inside having banished the person's soul and now inhabiting their body. Dressed in tattered strips of a three-piece business suit and with closely cropped hair, the Vamp had most likely been an attorney or banker before the Masters had begun their vampire war. Now, like so many other citizens of New Orleans, the man had been turned into a Vamp and guided by the hand of his Master.

The creature's eyes flashed brightly as it stared down at the boat.

Evelyn gasped and fell to her knees as if she'd been hit with a phantom punch to the stomach. The girls gathered around her as she held her hands against the side of her head.

"Get out!" She looked up to the sky, her eyes wide. "Get the *hell* out!"

"What's happening?" Kris asked.

"The Master of that Vamp is inside of her head." Alex felt the violation of Evelyn's mind through the Sight. "It's trying to turn her, corrupt her."

Scout looked from Alex to Evelyn, the leader of the Casket Girls now hunched completely over and rocking back and forth while moaning.

Alex grabbed the bow sitting at Zoe's side and nocked an arrow. She aimed at the Vamp's forehead, the spot right between his eyes.

Evelyn screamed, and Alex ignored the worried chatter of the other Casket girls in the boat.

She inhaled.

One shot.

Exhaled.

Fired.

The arrow tore through flesh, a direct hit as the shaft split the creature's skull. It fell backward with a thud, its orange eyes extinguished on the way down.

Evelyn gasped, drawing a breath as she dropped her hands from the side of her head. Alex handed Saw the crossbow before kneeling. Evelyn passed out, but Alex caught her, cradling the woman in her arms.

"Fuel line switched," Saw said. "Time to roll."

She hit the ignition button, and this time, the motor fired right up.

"Get us out of here, Saw," Alex said.

THE FLOODWATER HAD SUBMERGED the first story of the Creole townhouse, and the second level would also be under water in a few hours. Saw had sped out of the alley and through the French Quarter to get the surviving Casket Girls away from the Vamps.

They had to enter the home through the large French doors on the top-floor balcony which led into the home's master bedroom. Tall, leaded windows gave the suite a beautiful view of the city. A king-size bed sat against the far wall, and the dresser on the opposite wall had been trimmed in gold. It looked like the place had been restored to what it may have looked like in the 1800s, complete with massive oil paintings of plantation owners. From what Alex could tell, the place was vacant.

Wall and Zoe carried Evelyn inside, the woman still weak from whatever psychic damage the creature had inflicted upon her.

"Let's get her into another room and get away from these windows," Alex said.

The two women eased Evelyn down onto the bed in an adjoining room, setting her head down on the silk-lined pillows. Alex reached into her bag and pulled out a bottle of water.

"Drink," she said, pressing the bottle to Evelyn's lips.

Evelyn lifted her head and took a sip.

"Drink more."

Evelyn shook her head. "I'm fine. We have to ration."

Turning to the other girls, Alex said, "Scout and Kris, go search the other rooms and see what you can find. There might be some food or water in the kitchen. And make sure we're the only ones here."

They nodded and went to search the house.

"If you girls don't mind, I'd like to have a private word with Alex," Evelyn said, her voice soft and tired.

Alex sat on the side of the bed, watching the girls leave the room as Evelyn pushed herself up.

"Lie down," Alex said, putting her hands on her mentor's shoulders. "You need to rest."

Evelyn ignored Alex, sitting all the way up against the ornate headboard. Her eyes had gone bloodshot, her face pale. She reached out and touched Alex's cheek with the back of her hand, then smiled as she pulled away.

"What's the matter?" Alex asked. "What did that thing do to you?"

"I'm so proud of you."

Alex tilted her head. She opened her mouth but didn't quite know what to say.

"I am. Very much so. You've grown into such a strong woman, Alexandra. I saw it in you when I first took you in, but I never imagined you would become the woman you are today."

"Why are you telling me this?"

"Because you need to hear it. I don't tell you girls enough how I feel about you. Especially you. But know that everything I did, I did for a reason. I needed to keep you on your toes, make sure you didn't become complacent."

Alex noticed how Evelyn had switched to past tense. She shivered, even though the air in the room felt stuffy, stifling.

"Please, Evelyn. I don't understand."

Evelyn stared into Alex's eyes. "I need you to do something. For me. For your sisters. For the future of *humanity*."

"Of course. You know I'll do anything you ask me to do."

"Good, child. That is what I hoped you would say."

Alex huffed, shrugging. "What do you want me to do?"

"Kill me."

She sat back, her head swimming and her stomach in knots.

"What?"

"You're the only Casket Girl strong enough to do it."

"You've got to be kidding."

"I am not. It *must* be done."

Alex stood up. Keeping her eyes on Evelyn, she stepped back from the bed.

"Why? I don't understand."

"There's no time to explain. You must do it before the other girls come back, and more importantly before more of *them* come."

Alex shook her head. The first tear running down the side of her face.

"You can't expect me to do this. Especially if you aren't going to give me a reason."

Outside, a new explosion of feral screams roared through the city. Evelyn spun her legs around and slid off the bed, now standing before Alex.

"The Vamp in the alley got into my head. It connected me to the Master. He can now access all our research, our archives, everything. More importantly, very soon he will gain enough access to be able to see through my eyes. That puts you and the other girls in danger. I'm sure he's on his way here right now."

The screams came again, and Alex looked toward the bedroom door, hearing the girls yelling at each other from different rooms in the house. Evelyn reached out with her right hand and gently turned Alex's chin toward her.

"You have to do this, Alexandra. Right now."

Alex cried, doing her best to control the sobs rumbling through her chest. The others returned to the bedroom, all of them stopped in their tracks by the emotional charge they could feel in the room but not knowing why it was there in the first place.

"We have to leave this house," Wall said. "More of those things are coming."

"What's going on in here?" Zoe asked.

"I asked her to do it. For all of you. Remember that," Evelyn said, addressing the others. "Now, step out and close the door. Hurry."

"But what—"

"Now!" Evelyn screamed, interrupting Steph. "I love you all. Please, go."

Alex could see the emotions washing over Evelyn. She could feel the sorrow coming to the surface, and yet at the same time, Alex felt a deep evil emerging from deep within Evelyn's Sight. It festered and spread quickly through the woman's Sight like cold, dark motor oil.

Saw pushed the Casket Girls out of the room and pulled the door shut as Evelyn laid down on the bed. Alex stood over her.

"I love you, my child." Evelyn grabbed a pillow and moved it over her face.

"I love you, too," said Alex, leaning over and using both hands to push the pillow down.

"WHAT THE FUCK?"

Wall pushed past Saw and yanked the pillow from Evelyn's face. The woman's wide, dead eyes looked back.

The other girls filed into the room. Saw and Zoe stood on the other side of Alex. Saw looked from Evelyn's body to Alex twice, her mouth hanging open.

"I had to," Alex said. "She made me do it. For us."

"Liar!" Wall said, pulling a knife from her waist. "You power-hungry bitch!"

Wall lunged at Alex. Zoe ran at Wall, leading with her shoulder and knocking the larger woman to the ground. She dropped the knife, and Saw picked it up. Wall narrowed her eyes as she looked up.

"You killed her so you could be in charge."

"That's not true!" Zoe said, coming to Alex's defense. "I trust Alex. We need to hear her out."

"Why would she ask someone to *kill* her?" Steph asked. "That doesn't make any sense."

"Alex?" Zoe said, her face long and her loyalty to Alex teetering on the razor's edge.

Alex wiped tears from her face and looked around the room at what remained of the Casket Girls.

"In the alley, the Vamp got inside Evelyn's head. The Master was using it to get to her, to get to us. It was going to use her and kill all of us."

"Use her?" Kris asked. "For what?"

"To gain access to our archive. The Master could see through Evelyn's eyes."

"Bullshit." Wall stood up.

Outside, the creatures screamed.

"We don't have time for this now," Alex said. "If we don't stay together, we won't survive. I can tell you more later."

Saw handed the hilt of a knife to Wall. "You with us, or not? I believe Alex. I'd trust her with my life."

Wall stared at Saw, then back at Alex. "This isn't over."

"I know," Alex said.

Wall snatched the knife out of Saw's hand. Then she looked at Alex again.

"So what do we do now, 'leader?'"

The Casket Girls looked at Alex. Evelyn's warm body was still on the bed. Alex was now the one in charge, the one forced to make the decisions for the group.

"Evelyn believed the Master was after her. That it wanted to use her as a weapon in the vampire war against the other Masters. It had gotten in her head, so it must know now that she is gone. The Master will come for me next, as it might know that I have succeeded Evelyn."

"Then maybe I should snuff you out too, you know, 'save' us all?"

Alex turned to Wall. She understood why the woman felt betrayed, but this wasn't the time for explanations.

"The sun will be coming up. We need to get back to The Jimani as soon as possible and secure our archives. If the Master gets access to it, we're screwed."

"The Vamps were there, Alex," Zoe said. "They attacked us there already."

"They did, but they didn't yet know we had our archives stored in that building. I can't say for sure, but I don't think the Master got the location of the archive from Evelyn. As long as he doesn't get into my head, the archive's location is still hidden from the Master."

"Back to The Jimani to regroup. That sounds like a plan to me," Zoe said. "What do the rest of you think?"

Wall scoffed, her arms crossed. "What the fuck ever. She's in charge. Right?"

Wall walked out of the room, and the Casket Girls followed her except for Zoe and Saw. Alex lowered her head. She felt a hand on her shoulder, and then another.

"We trust you. Even if they don't," said Zoe.

Alex took Zoe and Saw's hands in hers. "Thanks."

An explosion outside rattled the glass in the French doors. The other girls came back into the room.

"They're coming," Scout said.

"We've got to go. Right now." Alex walked to the French doors with Zoe and Saw right behind her.

Steph pointed to Evelyn's body lying on the bed. "What about her?"

"I'm not just leaving her here," Wall said.

"There isn't time," Alex said. "We'll have to come back for Evelyn. The Master knows we're here. We have to leave now."

The Casket Girls walked past the bed on their way to the fire escape. Each one touched Evelyn's hand before wiping tears from their eyes.

Alex waited for the others to leave before looking once more at Evelyn's body.

"I won't let you down. I promise."

She closed the door and climbed down the fire escape to the boat.

———

FLAMES CREPT up the sides of several buildings on Canal Street as Scout navigated through the flooded streets below. The explosions punctuated the early morning hours, along with the occasional cry for help.

Saw wanted to keep her crossbow at the ready, so she handed the boat over to Scout. Alex looked around the boat and at the faces of her sisters. Scout kept her focus on the street ahead, while Wall, Steph, and Kris sat on the opposite side of the boat from Alex, Saw, and Zoe. Alex squirmed at the relative quiet, the only sound coming from the purring of the outboard motor. She wanted to talk, to mourn over Evelyn and have the girls reassure her that everything would work out. But that wasn't happening, and Alex thought the fact that Zoe and Saw sat next to her and on the opposite side of the boat from Wall and the others was not a coincidence. She didn't need the Sight to see the rift that Evelyn's sacrifice had created within the bruised remnants of the Casket Girls.

Fires still raged in many parts of the city. Though the sun's first rays had crept up over the Mississippi Delta, dark clouds hung on the early morning horizon, promising more rain which would bring more flooding. Without knowing if the city's pumps were running—and if they'd continue to do so—Alex realized that it wouldn't be safe in New Orleans. They'd have to leave. Soon.

"Shit." Saw stood up.

Alex snapped from her daydream and followed Saw's gaze.

The Jimani stood a block away, a blackened, charred hull of the building that had been their hangout and home. A smoky haze hung over The Jimani and what used to be the secret archive of the Casket Girls.

"So much for the archive," Wall said to Alex. "Looks like the Master didn't need Evelyn's eyes after all."

"The building was smoking when we ran. We don't know for sure that the Vamps knew the archive was here."

Alex could see the strain on Wall's face. The woman folded her arms on her chest and looked at Steph and Scout.

"This bitch ain't been telling us the truth. With Evelyn gone and The Jimani in ashes, I'm not sure there's much left of the Casket Girls."

"We can stick together, but this place isn't safe. Evelyn was training me with the Sight, and I might be able to access the archives using that power if I have some time to practice it. But that won't happen here, fighting the Vamps day and night. And if the Master gets hold of me, there's no hope."

Zoe and Saw nodded, but Wall stood up, spittle flying from her lips.

"This is my city. I'm not leaving. Ever. If you and your little bitches wanna run away with your tails between your legs, you go right ahead. Me, Kris, Scout, Steph—we're staying. We're defending New Orleans."

"We're stronger together than we are—"

"Oh, please," said Wall, interrupting Alex. "You weren't really gonna say that?"

Saw stepped between Alex and Wall, bringing her crossbow up. "That's enough. Alex is in charge of the Casket Girls, and she's calling the shots. It's what Evelyn wanted."

"Says Alex," Wall said. "We're not leaving, and you can't make us."

Alex extended her arm, pushing Saw's crossbow down. She looked at her friend.

"Wall is right. I can't force her to come with us." Alex scanned the boat. "But I can't stay here and take the risk of the Master getting hold of me like he tried to do with Evelyn. So I'm going to give you all a choice. This is your life, and you can do with it what you want. If you want to stay here with Wall, that is fine. But I am leaving. If you wish to come with me, then stay on the boat."

Kris and Steph followed Wall off the boat and on to the second floor of the building next to The Jimani while Zoe and Saw stayed with Alex. Scout hadn't moved. She sat by the motor, looking back and forth between Alex and Wall. After several moments, she shook her head.

"I'm sorry, Alex. Wall is right. This is *my* city. I can't let those fuckers take it over without a fight."

Scout stepped off the boat.

Alex watched as Wall, and the other girls went up the fire escape and into a building on Chartres Street. Scout stopped and turned around, standing before a blown-out window. She waved at Alex before running deeper into the building.

Alex put her arm around Zoe and nodded at Saw who backed up the boat before heading north through the city.

THE BOAT PULLED up next to Lake Pontchartrain Causeway.

"What now?" Zoe asked.

Alex shook her head. "I don't know. But I need time to work on the Sight, and I need to do it where the Master can't find me. I think we need to keep heading north."

Saw sighed. "Well, we got a long fucking walk ahead of us to get off this bridge. Unless maybe I can get one of these cars running. Either way, we should get the fuck out of here."

Alex took one last look at the New Orleans skyline, wiping a tear from her eye. "Someday, we'll return and take back our city."

Zoe and Saw nodded.

Alex squared her shoulders and put her chin in the air. "Let's roll."

ABOUT THE AUTHORS

Zach Bohannon

Zach Bohannon is a horror, science fiction, and fantasy author. His critically acclaimed post-apocalyptic zombie series, *Empty Bodies*, is a former Amazon #1 bestseller. He lives in Tennessee with his wife, daughter, and German shepherd. He loves hockey, heavy metal, video games, reading, and he doesn't trust a beer he can see through. He's a retired drummer, and has had a beard since 2003—long before it was cool.

For More Information
www.zachbohannon.com

J. Thorn

J. Thorn is a Top 100 Most Popular Author in Horror, Science Fiction, Action & Adventure and Fantasy (Amazon Author Rank). He has published over two million words and has sold more than 175,000 books worldwide. In March of 2014 Thorn held the #5 position in Horror alongside his childhood idols Dean Koontz and Stephen King (at #4 and

#2 respectively). He is an official, active member of the Horror Writers Association and a member of the Great Lakes Association of Horror Writers.

For More Information
www.jthorn.net

PHOENIX

BY LON E. Varnadore and Sam Korda

GREGORY MILLER SIGHED, took another long sip of beer, and sighed again.

"If it were anybody else, this thing would be on the back burner. But it's Emilia Andrews." The aging detective shook his head. He was slumped on the stool at the end of the bar, huddled in his wrinkled gray suit with his hair beating a steady retreat up his scalp. He'd been all set for a lovely weekend. The only work left in his caseload before last night had been putting together a few reports. Then he could cruise into Friday, pick up his daughter, Caroline, from the ex-wife's, and spend a couple days doing whatever she wanted to do. He'd even gotten it into his head that the two of them could go to dinner at their favorite spot, the one they'd gone to every Friday back when the three of them were all together. As he reached for the phone to make the reservation, the call had come through.

"Emilia Andrews, murdered," said the man sitting next

to Miller, shaking his head in disbelief. Remy was in many ways the opposite of Miller, a lanky, scraggly-haired guy in a ratty band t-shirt and jeans nursing a glass of wine. An artist who'd spent most of his time at Tulane smoking weed and conducting elaborate performance art pieces, mostly involving nudity. Getting stuck in a dorm with him had been one of the best things about Miller's college experience. All the other friends he'd made in school were criminal justice students whose idea of a wild night was getting another whisky ginger. Throughout those four years, Remy had kept Miller's horizons broad. This was why they still made a point of meeting for drinks every other week. A handful of times, they even got to catch up about things that didn't involve dead bodies.

"Shit, I remember reading an interview with her last week," said Remy. "She was on one of those lists, most influential entrepreneurs or whatever."

"They found her in the French Quarter," said Miller. "Some tourist stumbled on the body, but they must have just missed the perp because blood was still pooling from the stab wounds. Purse was gone. Franks thinks we can chalk it up to some dumb punk who didn't know who he was mugging and panicked. But..."

"But?" goaded Remy.

Miller shook his head.

"There's all these details that just don't add up. What was she doing in an evening gown by herself in a back alley on a Tuesday night? No signs of a struggle, and the guy took the time to slice her throat clean open *after* multiple strikes to the abdomen. We've got no leads on the purse at any of the pawn shops, and all the camera footage shows she was carrying what looked like a real Chanel bag. If it was some tweeker looking for cash, he probably would have dumped the thing quick. And they didn't touch her shiny silver necklace either."

"Hold up, you said cameras?" said Remy.

"A couple. Conveniently, none of them have direct line of sight on the scene itself. But we see her checking her phone, walking into the alley, some guy in a white hoody, gloves, sunglasses and a baseball cap follows her in. Couple minutes later, hoody guy runs out with the bag and buries himself in a crowd of drunk tourists. We're working the video forensics but still nothing. There are plenty of opportunities for him to ditch his clothes and become just another face. Interviews near the scene gave us precisely jack and shit."

"What about DNA?" asked Remy.

"What *about* DNA? You've been watching too much *CSI*," said Miller. He took a swig of his lager and stared into the drink's foaming abyss.

"There's something I'm missing," he said. "I can feel it. But I don't even know what I'm looking for at this point."

"Greg, I know you pretty well, right?" said Remy.

Miller cocked an eyebrow and nodded ever so slightly.

"Right," said Remy. "Trust me when I say I get it, man. I get why it's hard for you to accept how something crazy like this can happen. It's why you became a detective. Emilia Andrews was this town's Bill Gates or whatever. *I* even use Allokate and you know how much I hate social media and all that. It's fucked that one day, she could be walking around running a business and the next, she's dead on the street. But that's just the way it is sometimes. There's only so much order you can bring to chaos."

"Good point, buddy," said Miller. "'To Serve and Protect' doesn't have the same ring to it as 'Shit Happens.' Remind me to tell that to the guy who paints our squad cars."

"Look, all I'm saying is there's solving crimes and then, there's inventing mysteries," said Remy, throwing his hands up in a defensive posture. "Things don't always add up nice and neat the way you'd like."

"I guess," grumbled Miller.

The two friends sat in silence tending to their respective drinks. At the end of the bar, a pear-shaped man in an Ohio State jersey slammed another pair of quarters into the jukebox for a third consecutive play of "Sweet Home Alabama." Miller and Remy exchanged a glance well-honed through years of shitty parties. They finished off their drinks.

"What else you got going on tonight?" asked Remy.

Miller shrugged.

"Sleep."

"Ah, come on, it's only eight!"

"In case you can't recall, I have an early day tomorrow, what with the small matter of a murdered titan of business. A hangover's the last thing I need."

"We don't have to drink," said Remy, rubbing his chin with the palm of his hand. For a few seconds, he stared off into space lost in thought. Remy turned to look at Miller with a glint in his eye.

"Wanna see something cool?" he asked.

LE SPACE 29 was only technically a gallery. The warehouse by the docks had been lying dormant for years when a keen-eyed developer had swooped in and grabbed it for a bargain. They wasted no time converting the building into a hip art space. Their show wasn't opening for another four days and the cavernous space was shrouded in darkness.

Remy flicked a switch which turned on some string LED lights set up along the floor, outlining a path down the middle of the gigantic floor. The pieces flanked the two men as they walked towards a hulking shape that squatted off in the distance. Miller saw what looked like a pair of miniature skeletons set up on one pedestal, their intertwined forms represented by cut-up circuit boards. Across from them, a model of a DNA strand forged from gray metal snaked upward out of a papier-mâché hand.

"As soon as I heard the concept for the exhibit, I was hooked," said Remy, making a beeline across the warehouse.

As Miller toed his way down the lighted path, Remy fumbled with the thing at the end of it covered by a black tarp.

"Like, I'd had this idea for a while, but getting into this show was the kick in the ass I needed to do it," said Remy, his voice muffled.

"What's the exhibit about then?" asked Miller.

The shape under the sheet paused.

"Did I not tell you?"

"No," said Miller. "All you said was 'wanna see something cool.'"

"Oh. Oh, right! Sorry."

The shape resumed moving as Miller got closer and Remy kept talking.

"The exhibit's called *Multitudes*. It's about technology and how it affects interpersonal relationships. The whole idea that we're totally different people online than who we are in real life. And I've always had a bone to pick with social media. So, voilá…"

Remy stepped back into the light and pulled down the sheet.

"*Others*."

The contraption stood a head or so taller than Remy. It reminded Miller of those Terry Gilliam movies Remy'd forced him to watch in their college days. Most of the thing was taken up by a CRT screen—salvaged from an old TV, judging by the Panasonic logo—with a 90s' era keyboard sitting in a tray just beneath it. It was mounted in the center of a collection of wires, electronics, lights, and random doodads that only got more outlandish, the longer you looked at them. As Remy plugged in cords and flipped switches, more of the piece lit up. As they switched on, the machines contributed to a growing din.

"Holy shit," said Miller. "How long did this take you to build?"

"Couple of months. Really wasn't that hard, just spent a week or so going to yard sales and the rest of the time welding it all together. But hang on, 'cause we haven't even gotten to the best part."

Remy reached under the tray with the keyboard and wheeled out a small stool. Perching on it, he pecked at the keyboard.

"Putting all this crap together was the easy part. Ninety-nine percent of it's just for show. By the time I'd finished, it was only a week before the show opened. Nowhere near enough time for the coup de grâce."

"Which is?"

Remy raised his index finger and brought it down theatrically onto the keyboard. The screen crackled to life, the popping sounds of the old tube TV enhanced by additional noises from the small speakers. On a black background in white text was the word: OTHERS. Beneath that, a cursor blinked next to the phrase: "Press Enter to Generate."

"What really pisses me off about Facebook," said Remy,

spinning to face Miller, "is all the bullshit. And I know, real original, did I get that from Hot Topic, blah, blah, blah. But honestly, if this is where a lot of people have most of their social interactions instead of actually, y'know, *interacting*, people just keep posting random crap that's supposed to signal more about their own identity rather than start a genuine conversation, what's the point of even having real people on the site? Wouldn't it be just as valuable to have computers randomly generate people and what they say? You're getting the same value out of it either way, right?"

Miller could only shrug in the face of another onslaught of Remy-losophy. It was always easier to agree and let him get on with his planned remarks.

"I took that idea to its logical conclusion. The work uses an image generation algorithm to construct facial profiles from a range of statistically significant markers, then pairs that with a text-to-speech program that picks from a library of open-source texts and by this point, most people's eyes have glazed over like yours right now."

Miller blinked a few times before he caught what Remy had said. "What? Oh!" Miller chuckled. "I get it. The whole thing's a farce?"

"Not exactly." Remy fidgeted on the stool, rocking from side to side with his hands resting behind his head. "I just mean all the technical shit flies over my head, too. Like I said, I spent most of my time just building this thing. All the back end and coding stuff, I outsourced to a friend of a friend. All that bullshit is stuff he fed me, if anyone asks. The idea and the execution and everything is all me, but there's no way I'm learning to code just for this installation. Why do you think I majored in art?"

Miller nodded and looked back up at the machine. The noise from all the fans seemed less cacophonous than a second ago. It was settling into a rhythm. Like some beast was sitting in front of him, breathing heavily and watching his every move.

"Wanna try it out?" asked Remy.

"Sure," said Miller.

Remy leapt up and offered the stool to his friend.

Miller settled into it, staring at the blinking cursor. "All I have to do is hit Enter?"

"Yep!"

Miller tapped the key. The screen flickered and was replaced with one of the old spinning hourglass icons he recognized from the computer his family had when he was in high school.

"Right now, it's generating an identity," said Remy. "It's using a library of images that it has on a hard drive and mashing that up with information it's pulling at random from the Internet. That's also how it comes up with the phrase the person's going to say. It's a parody of a status update or a tweet..."

As Remy rambled on, Miller stared at the screen. The hourglass had disappeared. In the window that replaced it, pixels streamed in from off-screen. They came to rest haphazardly, forming the outline of a cheekbone here and a few strands of hair there. When the features of the face became more defined, Miller's heart dropped to his stomach. After thirty seconds, there was no mistaking the face he saw on screen.

"Remy," he said. His mouth was dry as a bone.

"Because ultimately it's—yeah?" Remy stopped mid-rant and turned to his friend.

"You said this thing makes up the people it shows, right?"

"Yeah. It's a commentary on artificiality."

Miller nodded. He'd had a long day. He didn't have the energy to ask why Emilia Andrews' face was staring back at him. All he could do was stare as her face resolved before him. The dead woman opened her mouth· and uttered a single word.

"Phoenix."

ONE SLEEPLESS NIGHT of frantic Internet searches later, Miller sipped coffee as he navigated his battered but serviceable green Ford 500 through the New Orleans suburbs. He pulled up in front of a squat house with a fresh coat of paint, just in time to see its owner kiss his wife goodbye on his way out the door.

"Morning, sunshine," said Miller's partner as he settled into the passenger seat. Albert Franks was just a couple years older than Miller, a fact belied by his weathered appearance. In the short time they'd been working together, the lines on his face had deepened and his waistband had expanded. The chain smoking didn't help either.

But while his body slipped by the wayside, his mind remained sharp as ever. When Franks called Miller on his bullshit, Miller listened. That wasn't the case with anybody else in his life. If it meant having to put up with the man burning through a pack of cigarettes a day, so be it.

"Which local pawn shop of ill repute are we hitting up first?" asked Franks as Miller pulled into the street.

"I did some digging on my own last night," said Miller. "Got a hunch, followed it, and I think we have a new angle we missed yesterday."

Miller passed a sheaf of printouts to Franks, a collection

of property listings and obtuse financial records. Miller'd taken care to circle in red the bits he needed Franks to see.

"Huh," said Franks after a minute of scanning. Then after a minute more, he followed up with an "A-*haaaa*."

"Yeah," said Miller. "The timing's a bit too perfect, right?"

"It's not nothing," said Franks. "You said a hunch got you here?"

Miller shrugged and made a show of staring at the traffic around them, avoiding his partner's gaze.

"Well, I figured if this wasn't random, there had to be a reason big enough someone would think murder was worth it. When I looked around and found all this, it fit the bill. If nothing else, we want to cover all our bases."

Franks nodded slowly. "Makes sense. Where we headed first?"

A GOOD DETECTIVE doesn't assume anything. Between the two of them, Miller and Franks had over two decades of experience in the NOPD and held themselves to this rule as much as possible. Even so, they were in no way surprised by *Allokate's* offices. The fledgling tech company had exactly the sort of open and hip office Hollywood had trained the two cops to expect. There didn't seem to be anyone working there who was a day over thirty, from the bespectacled guys tapping at computers to the perky young receptionist, Lucy.

She was the one who led the detectives towards the glass cube at the back of the building. There, hunched over a pair of monitors, was Michael Caulfield. Lucy smiled as she opened the door and made it a point to clear her throat.

"Mr. Caulfield?"

The young CEO jumped at his receptionist's voice. His eyes blinked rapidly as he re-acquainted himself with the real world.

"What? Hi! Yeah! Just a second." He tapped a few more keys then stood to greet the detectives.

"Good to meet you..."

"Detective Miller. This is Detective Franks. We spoke with you two days ago."

"Cool, cool. Have a seat, gentlemen. Thanks, Lucy. Wait!" The young woman hadn't even stepped towards the door when Caulfield caught himself, turning to the detectives. "Do you guys want anything? Coffee? Red Bull? Tea? Water?"

"Water would be great," said Franks.

Miller declined with a wave of his hand and got a good look at Michael Caulfield. For the past two years, the curly-haired college dropout's earnest smile beamed out from billboards and magazine covers. In interviews and press conferences, he came across as the typical tech wunderkind: intelligent, relentlessly analytical, and just awkward enough that you wouldn't be surprised if he revealed he was from another planet. There was a significant chunk of NOLA's movers and shakers who regarded him and the departed Andrews as messianic figures, here to bring forth the next great wave of post-Katrina revival.

You'd never guess that from looking at him now. Caulfield looked like he hadn't slept in weeks. Bags floated under bloodshot eyes. Scattered in between the robot figurines on his desk were mounds of crushed energy-drink cans. His rumpled black hoody featured a patchwork of multicolored stains and gave off a faint odor masked by liberal amounts of Febreze.

"So, just a water," said Caulfield. "And"

"Another Red Bull," offered Lucy. Caulfield nodded furiously.

"Exactly. Thanks, Lucy. Thank you so much." When she closed the door behind her, Caulfield collapsed in his chair and let loose a heaving sigh.

"Sorry if I zone out at any point here. I've gotten maybe six hours of sleep since... you know. And everyone's been so on edge. I'd take a sick day, but that'd probably make me go even crazier."

"So, you've been keeping busy," said Miller.

"Yeah. Nature of the beast. Silicon Valley isn't taking any time off. I could name dozens of companies that went bust because of way less than what we're going through. There was Flippo, Huntr, RejunkIt, CramJam."

"Mr. Caulfield," Miller said.

The young man seemed to experience a minor seizure. His upper body shuddered, and after a few more rapid blinks, he fixed his gaze on the detective. It was the sort of intense eye contact Miller hadn't experienced since he'd answered the door to a pair of Mormon elders.

"We've been reviewing our leads and evidence in the case. We just want to confirm a couple things with you."

"Yeah, yeah. Sure. Oh, thanks, Lucy!"

The receptionist had returned, passing a water bottle to Franks and a silver can to Caulfield. The entrepreneur cracked the top and started slurping down its contents like it was his first drink after days wandering the desert. Franks took a sip of his drink and made a show of withdrawing his notepad from his coat.

"So, on the night of the fourteenth, where were you exactly?"

Caulfield blinked again, his amiable grin frozen on his face as his eyes betrayed no real friendliness.

"I told you guys before, right? There was a meet-up that night. Bites and Bytes on Bourbon. I showed up around six, hung out all evening. Didn't hear about Emilia until after eight. My assistant pulled me aside, I was about to go up, so I was a little peeved by the distraction at first, but then... she told me..."

Caulfield's eyes fell to his desk. He raised the can to his lips and sipped as though on autopilot.

"Emilia was the glue. I've never been good at all that EQ stuff."

"EQ?" asked Franks.

"Emotional intelligence," said Caulfield. "Soft skills, all that. The company's running on my code, but if it weren't for her, we wouldn't have half the people working here that we do. We wouldn't even have the seed round that got us this office. That was all her. Keeping everybody happy and working together so the whole thing could hum along. Now, it's just me."

Franks turned in his chair to gaze at all the people in clear view of those working for the man sitting in front of him.

"Mr. Caulfield," chimed in Miller. "If you don't mind my asking, what *does* happen to the company now?"

Caulfield shrugged. "For now? We're still on track to launch our mobile app next month. But after that, yeah, I dunno. We're having an emergency board meeting Wednesday."

"And at that board meeting, do you have any idea what you expect to hear?"

"Um... no? I mean, I expect they'll want us—me—to start looking for a replacement for Emilia. Or maybe I shift from CTO to CEO and find someone to replace me. But I hope not. Coding's, like, the only thing keeping me stable these past couple days."

"You don't think you'll discuss Phoenix?"

Caulfield blinked just once.

"Phoenix?" he asked.

"Your new hardware division. Starting Q2 next year."

Caulfield started to speak, chuckled, frowned, bit his lower lip, and stared at Miller. His eyes fell back to the desk.

"Hey! Zuckerberg!" Miller snapped his fingers. "Phoenix?"

"We were going to announce that at that meet-up. Obviously never got to. How the hell do *you* know about it?"

"Property listings aren't classified, Mr. Caulfield," said Franks. "I understand you guys favor the unstructured office thing, but ten acres worth of real estate seems a bit much for a few beanbags and standing desks."

Caulfield's eyes darted back and forth between the two detectives.

"Oh. I get it now," said Caulfield. "And for the record, *fuck you*. Emilia and I have—had been planning the Phoenix move for years. Literally, years. What could I gain by killing her? Why would I murder the person I've worked with for five years to build this place from nothing? How dare you assholes even bring that up?"

"I didn't mean to offend, Mr. Caulfield. But we want to be sure we've got the facts straight."

"Well, excuse me then. Sorry for getting pissed when you imply an accusation of murder. I'll say it one more time in a way that might penetrate your thick skulls. I was at the meet-up. My assistant told me about Emilia. And for the past two days, I've had to walk into the office and face a void where my business partner and confidant should be and it's all I can do not to scream. That's about the size of it."

Caulfield's stare burned a hole into Miller's skull while Franks took pains to avoid eye contact with the man.

Miller offered an awkward cough. "Thank you for your time," he mumbled, standing to leave.

Franks was all too eager to follow his lead and the detectives strode across the carpeted floors of the office towards the exit.

On the elevator back down, Franks fidgeted with the buttons on his overcoat. A clear signal he was ready for cigarette number five of the day.

"You buy all that?" he asked Miller.

Miller sighed. "His reaction seemed genuine. But unless we get a better look at their books, there's no way to tell if he's telling the truth or if he stands to gain from Emilia's death."

"And the odds of us getting that info"

"Are about the same as striking oil in my backyard."

They didn't say a word to each other for the rest of the trip back to the car.

THE ANDREWS MANSION was constructed in the old French Colonial style, complete with white pillars framing a terrace stretching along the entire ground floor. The driveway was long enough for Miller to spend his time walking up it, calculating how many years he'd have to work to afford the lease on a place like this. By the time he made it to the mahogany front doors, he'd come up with a number in the triple digits. Miller knocked. There was no response. He knocked again.

"Mr Andrews, please, we have a few questions," he said to the door.

Franks was coming up the walk, sweating a bit from the heat of the day, fanning himself with his felt hat.

Bill Andrews came to the door, opening it until the chain of the door went taut. Miller saw the newly widowed man was even more disheveled than yesterday, his bleached blonde hair now an unruly mess framing his bloodshot eyes.

"Didn't I answer all of your questions?" Andrews asked, a small look of panic on his face.

Miller chalked it up to nerves and was glad Franks hadn't seen it. But then, Miller was still spooked by how Caulfield had taken the news when they dropped the word Phoenix. He wondered if Mr. Andrews knew anything about it.

Only one way to find out.

Franks came up and said, "Look, we really only want to ask one or two more questions and then, we'll let you go."

Franks gave Miller a look. Miller cocked an eyebrow and shrugged.

Like I know if it will work again? Miller thought, guessing what his partner was saying in a single look.

Franks looked at Andrews and then, Miller.

"How long have you been holed up here?"

"Two days. Why?"

"No reason," Franks said with a wave of his hand.

"I understand. Well, come in," Andrews said as he shuffled away from the door and let the two in, missing the silent exchange between the two partners.

Inside, the mansion was as it had been before, except for a few takeout containers scattered around. It was cooler, which Miller was thankful for since it was so humid out. Andrews walked towards the couch where they had done the interview two days before. He pushed a takeout carton with two beignets inside to the table. He then lifted them up to offer them to Miller and Franks. Miller shook his head, seeing that they weren't from Café Du Monde, not to mention they appeared to have hardened to the consistency of stone. It occurred to Miller those things could be days old. Franks mumbled something like "Thanks" and took one, bit into it, and showed he still hadn't learned how to eat one without getting powdered sugar everywhere.

Andrews settled back into the same spot as last time. He was still wearing the robe that they had found him in when they interviewed him before as well. It was dark, and Miller realized the blinds were all drawn. The smell of days'-old food and an unwashed body created a mélange he wished to be out of as soon as possible. It reminded Miller of when Remy wanted to see what a week without bathing was like. Miller shuddered and turned back to Bill.

"What can I answer?" Bill asked, his body hunched up and his eyes hollow.

"Do you happen to know what the word, 'Phoenix' might mean?"

Andrews' eyes grew wide for a moment. Miller noticed his breathing grew a bit more rapid.

"How did you hear about that?"

"New piece of evidence," Miller said.

He didn't need to know that Franks gave him a sidelong look. He felt his partner give him a stare for a beat.

"It was a business deal she and Caulfield were speaking about. I didn't get most of it. But, from what I understand, she was really gung-ho about it. And it worried me."

"Why is that?" Franks asked, leaping at Andrew's statement.

"It was a high risk for us. Emilia was always a high-risk, high-reward kinda girl. She almost broke her back heliskiing. She landed wrong and the doctors said had she landed at a slightly more acute angle, she'd have broken her spine."

Miller nodded, having seen the ME's report about the body.

"So, was she more for it or against it than her partner?" Franks asked, looking a little more interested in Andrews.

Andrews shrugged. "As I said, she was gung-ho about it."

"And yourself?" Franks asked.

"It wasn't something I wanted her to do. It was volatile. The idea of moving there, uprooting everything? It was too much of a risk." Bill's eyes grew more vacant and distant. "If it failed, she would have lost a large swath of the company and we'd be close to destitute."

Miller rolled around what he wanted to say for a moment, Franks looked like he was doing the same. He wanted to ask at least one more question before Franks did. Only one thing came to mind.

"How long was the pre-nup for?"

"It expired last year," Andrews said. "But, I'd never—"

"Yeah, yeah," Miller said. "Love of your life and all that."

Miller saw something in Franks' head spinning. He let his partner take the lead.

Yet, Franks nodded and said, "Thank you for your time. We will be in contact with you."

Franks nodded at Miller, grabbed his hat, and propelled himself to the exit. Miller guessed that even with his dulled senses, the smell was getting to him, too.

Outside, Franks looked at Miller. "I don't know about you, but I think he looked spooked. He probably did it."

"How are we going to prove it? He has a pretty solid alibi."

"Do you think that he was really at the meet-up? You know you can slip out of those without an issue."

Franks sparked up and looked at Miller. "I still think it's him and not that alien, Caulfield."

Miller's cell went off, and he read the text. "Payment, late. Please rectify."

Fucking bitch. He had once loved her. He still couldn't get over the passive-aggressive messages.

"Will do," he texted back. The two got into Miller's car and started off.

Miller looked at Franks while they sat at a traffic light, coming up on hour seven of what was turning out to be a long day.

"I think I owe you—"

"You think?" Franks asked, glaring at Miller. "I've been on this wild fucking goose chase and you have offered me zero explanation."

"It wasn't a goose chase. We got a reaction out of—"

"We got barely anything. The alien probably is at this moment preparing to sue us. The husband could be good for it. He also might be storing all his urine in jars in the basement, so really, who knows," Franks said.

The rotund cop settled back into the seat and sighed. After a handful of heartbeats, he rolled his eyes towards Miller.

"Show me," he said.

"Show you what?" asked Miller.

"Fucker, you know what. Show me. Now!"

"Stop smoking in the car and I will, asshole."

Franks took a long drag of the cigarette and blew it out of the window. Slowly, he rolled the window down and made a show of flicking the butt out. "Happy?"

"Stop smoking in my car," Miller said. "We're going now."

THE SHORT DRIVE to Remy's and the installation was still tense, neither Franks nor Miller saying anything on the drive down Canal towards the docks. When they pulled up to the building, Franks took one look at the place.

"Well, at least we aren't at one of the psychics at Jefferson."

"That was on a lark and you know it," said Miller. "Besides, the woman was right."

"She said a tall dark man is the key to your problem. She was doing a cold read on you," Franks said. "I worry about you sometimes, Miller."

"Miller? That you?" Remy came out the front door, dressed as before. His svelte frame leaned against the open door. "I told you, the thing isn't ready yet."

"I need you to show me and my partner."

"But, it isn't—"

"Remy, please," Miller said, walking up to Remy before Franks could ask a question.

"All right," Remy turned to push the other large door into its pocket and revealed the art exhibit. It was on, faces and words popping up randomly. The face of Emilia Andrews popped up, and she once more called out, "Phoenix."

"See?" Miller said.

"This is your smoking gun?"

"It gave me Phoenix. Both Caulfield and Andrews were—"

"Umm, what are you two guys talking about?" Remy asked, looking between the two of them.

"A case," Miller said. "Remy, your installation. I think it's channeling Emilia Andrews."

"The dead chick? No way. It's an algorithm, nothing more, man. Random generation. I told you that."

"No, it isn't," Miller said. "That is Emilia Andrews, and that is a word sent by her. This can't be a coincidence!"

"Miller, shut your mouth," Franks said, pulling Miller back. He nodded towards a college kid in a ratty t-shirt who was watching the three of them intently.

It was another employee of the gallery. The kid made a show of averting his gaze, then pulled out a smartphone and started to tap away.

"We're leaving!" Franks said.

"Why?"

"Cops at art exhibit commune with dead," Franks said. "This is a bad idea. We need to talk to the chief."

"Fine."

WHEN THEY GOT BACK to the station, Miller went to sit down when he passed a detective's desk. Two other detectives were there, laughing at something on the sleek new MacBook. Miller caught a clip of Franks shouting to him about leaving.

Fuck me, what happened.

He looked closer at the screen and realized the argument from not even an hour ago had already been posted on Facebook.

Shit!

Moments later, Chief Chavez called Miller and Franks

into his office. Miller could tell that the chief was pissed. As soon as they walked in, Chavez slammed the door.

"Get the curtains, Franks."

Miller's eyes glanced to the golden gloves trophy, set to one side to allow anyone who visited to know he'd won three years in a row.

Franks did as he was told, pulling the blinds down with one yank as Chavez walked back to his desk. The chief's forehead vein was pulsing, and Miller realized he and Franks might have been in too deep.

"What in the Holy Fuck is wrong with you two! Ghost stories? Accusing the vic's husband of doing it without a shred of physical evidence?"

"Chief, I'm telling you, the husband did it. His motive is crystal clear and his alibi's shot full of holes. Maybe if the CSI guys gave it one more pass—" Miller said.

"Miller, stop. The husband's lawyer's already screaming at me. And he is the pricey kind, the one with clout," Chavez said.

"Chief, we will find something," Franks said.

"No. You two are done. The Facebook bullshit of a ghost helping won't be good, but we can play it off as a one-time thing. You make asses of yourselves like this again, you are both coming in and your heads, fuck, *my* head might roll. Understood?"

"Yes, Chief," they both said.

Chavez sighed. "I want a report on my desk today. And get on the phone to the DA. I want a subpoena for that company, Allo-whatever. We need to look at their books and that kid Caulfield's stake in all this."

Miller frowned. "Why do we need all that?"

Chavez looked at him like Miller'd just asked why water was wet.

"So that we can get a warrant. You said it yourself yesterday, Caulfield's a weirdo. Can't get a read on him. And if he wants to be cagey with what exactly is going to happen with his company, then it's our job to kick the damn doors down. Metaphorically speaking."

"Sir, all due respect, but am I hearing you right? You're going after Caulfield. We know he was nowhere near the scene the night of the murder!"

"Jesus, Miller. Believing in ghosts is one thing, but this is a whole other level of naïve. You think a guy with Caulfield's money can't buy whatever he wants? I understand you've been at this awhile but believe it or not, I've been a cop a lot longer than you have. And I know this asshole's type. They think they're untouchable because they've got enough money to buy anything their measly little heart desires. Well, Caulfield isn't gonna code his way out of this one. All it takes is one solid connection we can shove back in his face and he'll fold. Seen it a million times."

Miller considered a snide remark about who was following hunches now, but Chavez's expression made it plain how suicidal that would be.

"Chief, Caulfield's innocent. He's not worried about money, he's worried about the company he's built. Andrews is the one who stood to lose something here."

"That's conjecture, and you know it, Miller. We'll know more when you go out there and get me that subpoena as ordered. This conversation is over. Stop chasing ghosts and do your jobs. Both of you."

Franks and Miller stood up and headed out the door. As they returned to their desks, the other detectives on the floor made a show of suddenly looking very busy.

Great, Miller thought. *We're already dead men walking.*

Miller looked at Franks. Franks stared at the caseload piled on his desk.

"Drop it, Miller."

"But—"

Franks looked at Miller. "Drop it. We have ten other cases. Let it drop."

"But you know Caulfield—"

Franks leaned across the desk, pulling his gaze up to match Miller's. "We were given a choice. My choice is to stay employed and not overreach. You want to kill your career, go with God."

Franks had a point. Miller was on the job ten years as a detective. And objectively, this was crazy. He was listening to something that was a fucking algorithm, according to Remy. He had his mortgage. He had a kid to support and an ex-wife hounding him for alimony. He needed this job.

He also had Andrews' reaction to hearing the word "Phoenix." The man had been so sure no one would stumble on that clue, and the panic he'd displayed made it clear Miller had been on to something.

Miller went over his options. He didn't have the trust of his partner. The chief was ready to shitcan him if he did anything other than follow his marching orders. All he had to do was stay at his desk, phone up the DA, and fill out reports for the other ten cases that they were close to clearing for Robbery-Homicide. Then it'd be quitting time. He'd head to the bar, grab a beer, forget about the chief willing to sweep everything under the rug to save his own neck and keep Bourbon Street pretty for the guidebooks so tourists from Bumfuck, Iowa, could keep showing up to drink their faces off...

He couldn't do it. Miller looked at his partner.

"I have to do this, Franks."

"Well, buddy, I like having a job that gets me real money. Makes paying bills a hell of a lot easier," Franks said without looking up. "So, you're doing it alone."

"I know."

"I'll hold off Chavez as long as I can if he asks what you're up to, but no promises."

"I owe you one, partner."

"Just be right about this," Franks said, looking up at Miller.

For a moment, Miller saw Franks' attitude. The message was clear.

It's do-or-die time, Miller thought.

He picked a file from the stack in front of him and started typing on autopilot, buying a little time as he plotted his next move.

"YEAH, I'M COMING!" came the muffled voice from inside.

As he stood on the stoop of the vinyl-sided house, Miller regretted not taking up his partner's habit. Not only could it warm him in the chill of the night, but a smoke could be just the thing to calm him down. His best-case scenarios for how this could play out involved a bunch of mandatory sessions with a shrink. On the other hand, he didn't need a psychologist to tell him what would happen if he went along with Chavez's half-assed farce.

The door creaked open, snapping Miller out of his reverie.

"Hey, Miller," said Remy, resplendent in gym shorts and a faded gray t-shirt. Even at three in the morning, he seemed wide awake. "Jesus, you look terrible."

"Great to see you too, man," said Miller.

His friend wasn't wrong. After a long day of going through the motions at work, he'd picked up Caroline from school and dropped her at the ex-wife's. Then he'd conducted more research. Since it wasn't technically during his shift, he figured there'd be no reason for Chavez to bite his head off.

His first tactic—investigating anything else he could find about Allokate's plans for Phoenix and the newly widowed Mr. Andrews' personal affairs—hadn't turned up anything. And there was no way he'd get another shot at interviewing Bill again. Three beers deep, he thought of Remy and his machine. This led Miller to fall down a deep Internet hole, researching everything from spiritualism to voodoo to accounts of supernatural experiences that featured too many words like "presence" and "ectoplasm." At last, he came up with something like a plan that deposited him unshaved and unwashed on Remy's stoop at an ungodly hour on a Saturday morning.

"I need to talk to you about your machine," said Miller. It was more like a croak.

"My machine?"

"The installation, whatever. *Others*."

"Oh! Okay, I guess. Come on in. Coffee? Whisky? Both?"

"Sure," said Miller, picking his way through the detritus littering the floor of Remy's apartment.

While Remy toiled in the kitchen, Miller sat on the artist's ratty old couch.

"How's that case going?" asked Remy. "The murder?"

"Got some leads."

"Right on, man! I guess it must be going good if you've got time to shoot the shit with me about art."

"Yeah, about that. When did you say that exhibit opened?"

"Monday." Remy made his way over to the couch with a steaming mug in each hand. "Want me to comp you a ticket? There'll be an open bar."

"I'll think about it. But right now, the thing is still just sitting there. Right? No one's touched it or anything?"

"I hope not. It'd be a bitch and a half to figure out how to fix that thing if anyone started messing with it. The guy who programmed it is from Benin."

"Where?"

"Country in West Africa, birthplace of voodoo if you can—"

Miller held his hand up as the alarm bells went off. *Just what I need.*

"How'd you connect with him?" Miller asked.

Remy shrugged. "Friend of a friend. This hacktivist I used to date hooked me up with this kid who's infamous in her crowd. Not for anything serious, mostly DDOS attacks on big corporations. He was way cheaper than any of the stateside guys I found."

"And this kid, what did he tell you about the program he cooked up?"

Remy squinted at his friend.

"I'm still pretty computer illiterate, so he just sent a few lines to parrot at people when they ask. Why the sudden interest in art? I know you're supposed to be nosy, but I think this is the longest we've ever spent talking about my shit."

Miller debated how to answer that question. It was the one he'd been dreading. Right now, Remy was the only one in Miller's circle of friends who wasn't convinced the detective had gone nuts. The nagging voices in the back of his mind were imploring him to listen to reason. When was the last time the guy ranting about the paranormal and citing websites with titles like "The TRUTH about GHOSTS CRYPTIDS AND DEMONS that they DONT WANT YOU TO KNOW!!!!!" had been onto something?

But he couldn't shake it. Emilia Andrews had appeared to him. Her ghost in the machine had given him an actual, workable clue. Even if it was the only thing he had to cling to at this point, it didn't change the fact it was true.

Miller took a deep breath.

"Remy, do you remember earlier today when I said your machine generated Emilia Andrews? That word she said, Phoenix. I don't think that was random..."

JUST AS BEFORE the warehouse was dark. Miller could only shift from one foot to the other as he watched Remy fumble with the equipment and wires the two of them had spent most of Saturday crossing New Orleans to acquire. The exhibit was a bit more put together since his last visit. This time, the lights didn't end at Remy's installation. They were splayed out all over the floor. Some of the strings doubled back on themselves. Others were placed in strange looping patterns. At odd intervals, Miller thought he recognized designs in their arrangement.

"All set!" declared Remy after what felt like hours.

Miller turned to look back at the installation. He'd been tuning out Remy for almost the entire night since he'd dropped his bombshell about what his installation was really doing. His artist friend had no shortage of opinions on what all of this really meant, and he'd related them at length. Miller had nodded along to Remy's technobabble as best he could since that enthusiasm was the only thing that got them this far.

"Speak into this," said Remy, holding a squat gray microphone towards Miller.

"That's it?" asked Miller. He eased himself back into the stool which creaked under his weight.

"There was a plug for the cord so I figured, why not give it a shot?"

Miller stared at Remy.

"Seriously?"

"Dude, what do you want from me?" asked Remy. "I have as much experience with ghost computing as you do. The inputs should hook into the main machine. If it doesn't work, I've got the number of a witch doctor we can try."

"Okay, okay," said Miller, waving him off. "Boot it up. It can access old stuff, right?"

"Yup. All the iterations should be stored on the hard drive. The idea was to make a mosaic of all the randomly generated identities. Then I superimpose that next to a bunch of real profile pictures to show how—"

"Remy?"

"Yeah?"

"Shut up."

"Okay."

The machine whirred to life. This time, sitting in the driver's seat, it felt even more like the thing was alive. Remy navigated through menus to the archive. When he found the correct file, he hit Enter. The screen went dark. Pixels flew in from out of frame. In less than a minute, Emilia was back. She seemed more haggard than Miller remembered, like she'd aged decades in a couple days.

"What happened to her?" asked Remy.

Miller shrugged. He flicked the power switch on the mic.

"Emilia? Can you hear me?"

Emilia's eyes went wide. Her dismay was replaced by shock.

"Emilia…"

Her voice crackled through the speakers. It echoed in the air of the huge and empty warehouse.

"Holy fuck," whispered Remy.

"Emilia, I'm Greg Miller. I'm a detective."

"Detective?" Emilia's face darkened with an accusatory glare. "Murder. *Murdered*."

"Yes. Uh, Mrs. Andrews, I'm trying to find who… well, who killed you. But I'm running into problems."

"See. See me." Each word seemed like a struggle for her. Like she was using muscles she hadn't exercised in years.

"Mrs. Andrews, I need your help."

"Help."

"Did your husband murder you?"

"Who?"

Emilia cast her gaze to the side. He could tell she was trying to remember, but the longer the pause grew, the more Miller's heart sank. If this was the end of the road, he found that more depressing than if he'd never encountered her ghost at all.

"I talked to Caulfield."

Hearing the name of her business partner brought a forlorn smile to her face. She still stared down at some point Miller couldn't see.

"I also went by your house and spoke to Bill—"

Emilia looked directly back at Miller. There hadn't been any interval. One second, she'd had that mournful gaze, and the next, she peered back out of the screen with pure rage on her face.

"Bill. Murdered. *Murdered*. BILL MURDERED."

Her voice filled the building. The tiny speakers above

the monitor didn't look like they could achieve such a loud volume. Her shouting felt close to deafening. Miller had to cover his ears.

"BILL MURDERED! MURDERER! BILL! BILL! BILL –"

Emilia's voice rose into an unbearable cacophony. The ghost screamed her husband's name, a chant where each word felt like a dagger stabbing anyone within reach. Miller wondered how loud a sound had to be to burst eardrums.

At last, mercifully, the screen went dark. The machine quieted. Remy poked his head around the side of it, an unplugged extension cord dangling from his hand.

"You good, man? The thing was obviously stuck in a loop. Wanted to save it before it fried anything. Or we went deaf."

Miller nodded, rubbing his sleeve on his brow to mop up the sweat. He let out the breath he didn't know he'd been holding.

"I think we've got our man," he said.

———

MILLER LOOKED at the door of the Andrews' home. The sun wouldn't rise for another couple of hours, and in the darkness before dawn, the imposing bulk of the mansion seemed to leer at him.

The evidence was there. The ghost of Emilia Andrews had accused her husband. But how was he supposed to use that? There were so many ways this could go where he ended up with no job and multiple appointments at the county courthouse.

He called Remy. It rang four times before finally, his friend answered.

"How fast can you move the installation?"

"Why?" asked Remy, annoyed and groggy. The impromptu all-nighter had clearly taken its toll. "You know this has lots of tiny moving parts, right? Do you have *any idea* how long it took to track down—"

He hung up before Remy continued. Miller didn't have time to scream at him. He sighed and walked towards the mansion.

"If you can't get Muhammad to the Mountain... the Mountain will come to Muhammad," he said. Miller wasn't sure that was how it worked. He didn't care.

For the third time, he crossed the driveway. Standing before the door, Miller took a deep breath. He raised his fist and knocked.

Bill Andrews' all-too-familiar bathrobe now sported a pair of fresh mustard stains. Half his hair stood straight up from his scalp and it seemed like focusing his eyes was proving difficult. He also reeked even more than before, a feat that shouldn't have been possible. You could make the case that the man was trying for suicide through sheer neglect.

"Detective?"

"Hello, again, Mr. Andrews," said Miller. "Sorry to bother you so late, but new details have emerged. I need you to come with me."

"Excuse me? I'm not going anywhere this late!"

"It should just take a few moments down at the station."

Miller always had been terrible at lying. Bill Andrews snorted.

"If you can show me a warrant, then fine. If not, we have nothing more to discuss."

The widower made to close the door. Miller stepped forward, doing his best not to wince as the heavy mahogany pressed against his loafers.

"Look, detective, I've been having a rough couple of days," said Andrews. Fury and disbelief started to color his expression. "So, I'm going to kindly ask you to get your ass off my property before my lawyers destroy you, your fat-ass partner, and anyone else in your department I can get my hands on."

"Okay," said Miller. His hands shot forward and grabbed Bill by the lapels, yanking the man out of his house and towards the Ford.

"What the fuck is this? Aren't you supposed to read me my rights?"

"Yeah, if I was arresting you," said Miller. He slammed Andrews onto the car and withdrew his cuffs from inside his coat. The man offered no resistance, so it was easy for Miller to go through the all-too-familiar motions.

"But I'm not arresting you," said Miller. As he maneuvered Andrews into the backseat, he found himself speaking at Remy-esque speeds to bullshit his way through the situation. "I'm detaining you, which I can do without cause for up to twenty-four hours."

"That's not how this works!" shrieked Andrews as Miller slid into the driver's seat. "That's not how any of this works!"

Miller flipped on the radio. Jabbing at the dial, he landed on a channel blasting guitar riffs under the guttural singing of a man who must have despised his vocal cords.

Not my first choice, but it beats the peanut gallery.

As he peeled out of the mansion's driveway, Miller twisted the volume knob all the way up as Andrews screamed his head off in protest.

"THIS ISN'T the goddamn police station! What the fuck is going on here?"

As he pulled up to the warehouse, Miller's heart caught in his throat. Waiting next to a tan sedan was a nervous-looking Franks. Next to him was Chavez. Miller had made the call to his partner on the way over, but the captain was most definitely not supposed to be here. The leash on Franks must have been tighter than he'd thought. The chief's face was bright red, and the small man was practically hopping from foot to foot with suppressed fury.

"What the hell is wrong with you?" Franks said as Miller stepped onto the curb. As he got closer, his voice dropped to a whisper.

"Chavez figured you'd try something like this. I tried to keep it under wraps, but when I went to leave middle of my shift—"

"Okay, okay," said Miller. "Don't worry. This is all me."

Chavez watched this interaction looking like he was about to pounce on Miller, his hands balled up and ready to swing. He still hadn't said anything. Miller found this even more terrifying than the usual stream of invective. Miller stepped towards his boss, Bill Andrews in tow.

"He did it," said Miller. "I can prove it."

Chavez shook his head. It was a slow, deliberate motion where his eyes never left Miller. Franks took this as his cue and reached for Andrews, beckoning towards Miller. Against all his better judgment, Miller handed over the keys and Franks unlocked the cuffs.

"I am sorry, Mr. Andrews, I'll take you home and—"

Something behind Chavez caught Miller's eye. The darkened interior of the warehouse lit up. The string lights had turned on. Then there was the rumble of the garage door sliding open. Chavez shot an accusatory glare at Miller, who could only shrug in response. Franks squinted, trying to pick out anyone in the shadows.

"Hello?" he called.

The response was a low whirring that was too familiar to Miller. Chavez spoke.

"Miller, I don't know what you've been cooking up—"

"Sir, I swear to God I'm not doing anything," said Miller.

The screen on Remy's machine flickered to life. There was no title screen, no hokey loading animation. Just the scowling face of Emilia Andrews. If she'd looked older before, then she appeared downright skeletal now. Her eyes bulged out of her face, staring directly at her husband.

"BILL!"

"Oh, Jesus, no," whispered Bill Andrews.

"What did you do, Bill?" Emilia Andrews' voice boomed out of the machine, echoing in the massive space. "Why would you take our future away from us?"

"You were the one taking it away! You were willing to risk everything we had, everything we'd built!"

Emilia made a noise like a rasping cough. It was the closest she could get to a laugh.

"What *we'd* built?" She barked out another laugh. "Me, Bill. ME! I built! You MURDERED!"

Everyone looked to Bill. The man's indignation was replaced by a look of sheer panic. All three cops knew that look all too well. Bill stammered but couldn't form any words. Emilia's voice rang out again.

"Bill Andrews murdered! Murdered! Bill Andrews—"

"Shut up!" shouted a distraught Bill.

Emilia kept screaming her accusation. Bill growled and —before anyone could react—jammed his elbow into the transfixed Franks' nose. As Franks stumbled, Bill reached for the detective's waist.

Oh, shit, Miller thought.

It was all he had time to do as Bill grabbed Franks' handgun, spun on his heel, and fired three rounds at the face of his dead wife. His shots hit the console below the screen, the installation falling silent after a flurry of sparks. As Chavez and Miller reached for their sidearms, Bill turned to aim the gun at the chief. Everyone froze.

"This clown show is over," said the widower.

Miller could see the man was running on adrenaline and fear. The hand holding the gun was shaking, but at this range, Chavez was a hard target to miss.

"All this is going to go away or I will personally ensure your lives are over."

"Sure thing, Bill," said Miller. "Can't pin murder on you anymore. Now there's just the small matter of stealing an officer's weapon and then threatening—"

"Are you trying to be funny right now?" Bill swung the gun around to point at Miller, who did his best to maintain a stoic expression. "*I* am in charge here! I can buy and sell you idiots ten times over! I can shoot all three of you right now and walk! I can—"

Chavez had been out of the ring for many years. Though his physique was past its prime, his technique aged like fine wine. As his fist collided with Bill Andrews' solar plexus, the man staggered back, the wind knocked out of him.

Miller's partner leapt into action to reclaim his sidearm. When the detective's hand clamped on the gun, Andrews appeared to get a second wind. Wheezing, he let his animal instincts take over and clung to the pistol with a death grip.

Chavez drew his gun just in time for Bill to reorient himself, placing Franks between him and Chavez. As Miller fumbled for his own gun, it became clear Franks was fighting a losing battle. Even mad with fear, Andrews had more raw strength than the older detective.

Bill lifted his foot and jabbed it into Franks' calf. He fell to one knee as Bill brought the gun down to rest on Franks' scalp. Bill's eyes flared and the muscles in his hand tensed.

Three more shots rang out. When the sound faded, Miller realized they'd come from his gun. All he'd needed was to see his partner at the mercy of a killer. Training took care of the rest.

"Franks," he called out between deep, steadying breaths. "You okay?"

"Yeah," grunted his partner.

Miller stepped forward, his gun trained on the prone Bill Andrews. The man lay still, face frozen in a mask equal parts rage and terror. As he helped Franks to his feet, Miller looked to Chavez. The captain started to say something then closed his mouth. He sighed.

"Call it in. Then go home and see your kid. I'll take it from here."

"Thank you, sir," said Miller.

"Just another boring weekend," grunted Franks.

Miller chuckled, grateful his partner was still alive to make dumb remarks.

Holstering his gun, Miller was about to turn for his car when something caught his eye. *Others* flickered. For the briefest moment, Emilia Andrews smiled out at him, and he could've sworn she was grinning with satisfaction. Then, the screen went dark for good.

ABOUT THE AUTHORS

Lon E. Varnadore

Lon E. Varnadore is a science fiction and fantasy writer, spinning stories of military science fiction and science fantasy. Loves jazz, classic rock. You can keep tabs on Lon through the interwebs through website, twitter or The Facebooks. www.lonvarnadoreauthor.com/index.php/free-stuff

Sam Korda

Sam Korda is a science fiction writer living in New York City. When he isn't furiously smashing his keyboard to make words come out he's working with his best friend and sister on their video production company Galaxy Man Productions. If he had to pick a favorite food it'd be fried pork dumplings.

THE AMULET

BY SHIRLEY HARTNETT and Kim Petersen

THE RATTLE SHOOK Lillian with an echoing staccato as her world collapsed. She opened her mouth to scream, yet her words failed to penetrate the deafening silence. Strands of honey-blond hair clung to her sweaty forehead as she turned and spotted the old, rusted, iron gates of St. Louis Cemetery, her body rolling off the car's hood after shattering the safety glass.

It was supposed to be an ordinary afternoon as she strolled through the French Quarter of New Orleans on her way to the Creole cottage she shared with her husband, William. But what was happening now felt anything but normal.

The vibration stopped as suddenly as it had started, and an unusual silence fell around her.

I'm okay, she thought, forcing her eyes open and her limbs to move. *I'll just call William. He'll know what to do...*

As she tried to lift herself from the rough surface of the

road, she noticed her body becoming heavier, as if attracted to the asphalt like a chunk of lead to a magnet. She willed her legs to move, her heels scraped slightly against the hot road and she realized her brown sandals were no longer on her feet. A warm breeze cut through the stuffy air, and she felt her white summer dress shift against her skin. Her head became foggy, her fingers twitching as she fought to stay focused. She tried to blink before drowning in a sea of black, suffocated by an oppressive cloud of darkness.

A wail cut through Lillian's thoughts, pulling her from oblivion and back to the real world. But something felt different. No longer could she feel the weight of her body, nor the pain of getting hit by the car. She gazed at the scene with a sense of detachment, watching the paramedics, police, and hysterical people running around the intersection. Staring in wonder, she felt her body levitating. As she floated toward the sky, she saw everything. A feeling of eternal possibility swept over her, and with it came a clarity and serenity like she'd never felt before.

"We're losing her," a female paramedic said, glancing over her shoulder toward her partner. "Bring the defibrillator!"

Lillian hovered over the team of paramedics treating her mangled body. She felt their desperation and then a sense of hopelessness as they realized the woman could not be saved. Lillian wanted to reach out and tell them it was okay, to let them know William would be coming to take her home.

The paramedic sighed and shook her head as she wiped the sweat from her brow with the back of her hand. "She's gone."

Lillian panicked. *I'm not gone, I'm right here!*

She reached for the woman's red hair before looking

down again at her own motionless body, bloody and mangled on the road.

Lillian's luminous, green eyes were closed. Thick lines of blood ran across her cheeks and the skin had been savagely torn from her face. Her blond hair had been fanned out beneath her, mixing with the blood pooling on the road. She barely recognized herself.

A jolt. Then a sense of tearing, like something was being pulled from her. As she looked down upon her dead body, she couldn't bring herself to leave. William was coming— she couldn't go now.

A Ford F-150 came around the corner on screeching tires, stopping near the grisly scene. The truck door slammed, and he ran toward her, ignoring the paramedics and pushing the police out of the way. William—her beloved husband.

They had married the year before on a bright November afternoon. A simple ceremony in Jackson Square where they had met. She would never forget her wedding day— she vividly remembered the flutter in her heart as she approached the iron gates. Her pulse had been racing with the beat of the blues band playing in front of the St. Louis Cathedral. She clutched at her autumn sage and silver bell bouquet, stepping over the threshold and willing herself not to break out in a sweat. Then she spotted William. He stood beneath an old oak tree, wearing a dark suit to complement his smooth, olive skin and luxurious black hair. The moment their eyes locked, her pulse calmed. As she neared him, she felt a tingle run down her spine and to her toes as she basked in the love radiating from his sparkling, dark eyes.

But now, he fell to his knees. His breath labored, tearing and catching in his throat while he cradled her head and howled her name over and over. "No, no, no," he muttered, shaking off the red-haired paramedic in her attempts to comfort him.

"Don't touch me!" His dark hair covered his eyes, his sweat and tears mingled with her blood as he leaned over her lifeless body.

His lips quivered against her ear while he rocked her back and forth, sobbing. "Please. Don't. Leave. Me. You can't. We're in this together, remember? Our life together. The family we have yet to start. You're every little part of me. Breathe, Lillian!"

"Sir, please," the paramedic said to William as she tried to help him without getting too close. "We need to move her. People are crowding around."

William looked away from his wife. He gazed at the woman, shaking his head.

"I can't leave my wife. You have to bring her back!"

His face contorted, his eyes darkening. His whimpering became a deep growl. "Bring her back to me. Do you hear me? Save her!"

The paramedic shook her head. "I'm sorry, sir. There's nothing more we can do."

A few police officers closed in.

"Sir, we're going to need you to move away from your wife. You can accompany her in the ambulance to Tulane Medical Center."

Cursing under his breath, he stroked Lillian's face with two fingers before getting to his feet. William looked past the officers before speaking again to the paramedic.

"If you can't save her, then I'll do it myself." He pushed past the woman and climbed into his truck, slamming the door shut and speeding off.

Lillian's heart lurched as she watched him drive away.

"William, I'm still here," she said, her voice echoing in her ears.

She felt the force again, her body ascending faster than it had before and drawing her up into the sky. Lillian tried to resist, but she couldn't stop it.

She couldn't leave William. Not now. Their life together had only begun.

WHEN GRACE SPOTTED the couple emerging from the building, she dropped behind the wheel of her car, the camera with a telephoto lens poised loosely in her hands as she zoomed in on the wealthy stockbroker and his much-younger companion. She clicked a few times before reaching for her miniature camcorder, hitting the record button just in time to capture the balding millionaire sliding a hand up the woman's miniskirt and then pulling her in for a sloppy kiss.

"Ewww," Grace muttered with a grin. "You're awfully stupid for a savvy businessman, Mr. Finnegan."

Grace filmed the couple until they climbed into a black Mercedes, then tossed her camcorder on the passenger seat and started her car—ready for pursuit. Her client, Mrs. Finnegan, would be rather pleased with the evidence she had gathered to support the woman's case for divorce.

Grace frowned as she pulled away from the curb.

Or would she be pleased?

Even after a decade as a private detective, she could never really tell how people would react when presented with proof of a cheating lover. Long ago, she had acquired a don't-give-a-shit attitude about her clients and their motivations. Things were different when she had first started out.

Back then, she thought she could help make the world a better place. It wasn't long before her chosen profession tarnished her worldview. Case by case, she realized people were mostly distrusting, over-indulgent, cheating assholes.

She slid up from behind the wheel of her BMW, tossing her black hair from her face and pulling on her oversized sunglasses as she tuned her wireless CB radio to the police channel.

Her entire life, Grace had men falling over her. With her piercing blue eyes and shoulder-length hair as dark as midnight, she could flash a smile and get into crime scenes that were off-limits to other PIs. Grace belonged in the French Quarter—tattoos on her wrist, black boots, and ripped jeans. And any man stupid enough to make an unwanted advance would find out how much power she packed into a lithe, 5'8" frame.

Reaching for her coffee, she listened as she navigated the streets of the French Quarter, ignoring the occasional blasting horn, and profanities hurled from drunken pedestrians while she tailed her quarry.

A croaky voice came through the radio, immediately catching her attention as she recognized the make and model of a truck that happened to be at a scene of a fatal accident on Basin Street.

William.

Her eyes widened beneath the sunglasses as her mind whirled, and she almost choked on the coffee, spilling the hot liquid down her blouse.

"Shit!"

She pulled the car to an abrupt halt, glancing at the Mercedes as it disappeared around the next block.

"You're gonna have to wait, Mr. Finnegan."

She reached for a tissue and her cell, tapping William's contact while blindly dabbing at her blouse.

Please be okay, please be okay.

She had already lost him once. To *her*. She couldn't bear to lose him again. Her thoughts spiraled as she waited for a response. Her chest tightened with each drill of the ringtone. When he answered, his voice cut through like shards of glass.

"She's gone, Grace. Just like that. She left me."

She was silent for a second, her head buzzing while she processed the information. A warm, tender feeling ran up her spine and wrapped around her heart. She gasped.

"William, I'm so sorry. You know I'm here for you, right? Where are you?"

He pushed words through the phone.

"I'm at the hospital." It sounded like he'd stifled a sob. "No. I can't accept this. She can't just leave! I won't let her do this to me. To *us*."

"I know, honey, I know."

He continued to babble and sob, and yet she couldn't suppress her feelings for him. *William.* The brooding, dark man she had fallen instantly in love with years before—the only man to ever magnetize her heart. He would've been hers if Lillian hadn't waltzed in and stolen him away from her.

Grace said all the right things and comforted him as he grieved his dead wife. However, she couldn't help but allow a tiny glimmer of joy to wash over her heart as she contemplated what this could mean for her. The man she loved was free again.

GRACE DUMPED her backpack on the sofa and headed toward her Spanish Colonial kitchen to make some tea. She had been living smack-bang in the middle of the French Quarter for several years now, and she loved it. She adored the energy of this town, and she was sure it was a vibe she'd never outgrow. The history of New Orleans had seduced her at the onset—a place where the past and the present seem to coexist in harmony, as if neighbors with only an invisible veil between them. She had never indulged in the haunting ghost talk that surrounded the town, preferring to take a more practical line of thinking.

I'll believe it when I see it.

And after a decade of living here, she had yet to experience anything remotely paranormal.

She hit the kettle button and pulled out a mug, allowing the low noise of the boil to tune out her thoughts as she rotated her broad shoulders and stretched. It had been a long night. After talking to William, she had rushed to be by his side and help ease his burden. He had been a mess. Babbling all night long about finding a way to bring Lillian back. She had carefully played the part—consoling him until the Valium pulled him into a deep sleep.

Running her fingers through her shoulder length, jet-black hair, she knotted it at the nape of her neck and set out to pour the hot liquid into the mug. A raspy scratching sound coming from the living room caught her attention. She paused. Kettle poised mid-air, her nose wrinkled as she listened. Silence drifted through the air. Her blue eyes narrowed and then she shrugged as she set the kettle down and stirred her tea. She needed sleep.

Cradling the mug, she padded toward her upstairs bedroom. As her foot touched the first step, the scuffing noise began again. Her head whirled in the direction of the sound. Her vision focused on the archway leading into the living room.

What the hell?

The house was old, and she was used to the groans and creeks brought on by the humid, Louisiana weather, but this sounded abrasive—as if someone or something were deliberately scratching the floorboards. A rat, perhaps?

Placing her mug on the step, she backtracked and crept toward the sound. As she neared the living room threshold, her pulse raced.

Argh! Stop being a pussy, she chastised herself.

Still, she was having trouble ignoring the icy tingles at the base of her neck. Peeking around the doorframe, she froze, and a sharp breath tore through her lungs.

A mist-like substance filled the corner of the room, hovering above the floorboards. Grace mouthed words she'd never say out loud in front of her mother and clutched at her chest. She closed her eyes and furiously shook her head, stepping back into the hall.

It can't be. I'm hallucinating.

She took a few deep breaths and tangled her fingers together until her knuckles grew white before peeking into the room again. She blinked. Once. Twice. The vapor had dissipated, and her living room now appeared normal. She laughed out loud and turned toward the stairs again.

"God, I'm a kook," she mumbled, picking up her mug and dragging her feet upstairs.

When she saw her big, plump bed waiting for her, she flung herself under the sheets and closed her eyes. Grace fell asleep while the cream in her mug filmed across the surface of the tea.

GRACE BLINKED. She frowned as the sound of a banging window shutter woke her from a deep sleep.

Odd, she thought, getting up to look around. She didn't have any shutters on her house.

She trampled through the house on stiff legs, looking in closets and behind curtains. The clanking stopped before she could find the source.

Since she was already up, she decided a strong cup of coffee was in order. She scrubbed her face, threw on her casuals, and walked a few blocks to her favorite café, the Café Du Monde at the French Market—an old-school joint serving the best chicory coffee and beignets in New Orleans.

Grace greeted the elderly man behind the to-go counter with a tired smile.

"Extra strong this morning, Jimmy," she winked. "I'm going to need all the help I can today."

He retuned her smile with a twinkling grin. "Ahh. One of those nights, Miss Grace," he said knowingly.

She rolled her eyes and groaned.

"Get your mind out of the gutter before the street cleaners come and collect your ass."

Grace took her coffee and donuts from Jimmy's hand and then flopped into a nearby chair, scanning Jackson Square across the street. She sighed when her eyes stopped on a lush banana tree in the far corner. The memory of William and Lillian exchanging vows the year before tormented her. She had turned down the gold-leafed invitation that arrived in her mailbox weeks before the wedding. Yet, unable to contain some twisted inner urge to punish herself, she had mingled with the Saturday crowds and lingered along the park edges during the ceremony, stifling the sobs tearing through her heart.

Nodding at Jimmy on her way out of Café Du Monde,

she began the walk home while contemplating the sudden change in William's life. Sure, he'd need time to mourn and recover from Lillian's death—she would give him all the time in the world. After all, she wasn't going anywhere. And when the time was right, just maybe, they could pick up where they had left off before Lillian had swooped him up like a swindling thief.

As soon as Grace entered her house, she knew she wasn't alone. The hairs on the back of her neck went up with a tingle. She crept to the kitchen while her ears heard the clanking again. It seemed to be coming from upstairs. Setting her coffee on the table, she cautiously headed for the stairs.

With each ascending step, Grace's mind whirled like a hurricane as she struggled to figure out who or what was in her house. The sound grew louder. She ran down the hallway and made a quick dash into her bedroom. She slid her hand under her pillow and retrieved her gun—an old habit developed as a P.I.

The noise shifted and now sounded as if it was approaching her room—a gnawing bang against the floorboards taunted her as it relentlessly drew nearer. A sharp breath tore through her lungs and her dark hair clung across her face as she spun around toward the opened door. She waited until the intruder was close. She dropped to one knee behind her bed and raised the gun.

Suddenly, the clanking stopped, and the house went utterly silent. Grace's senses flew into overdrive as she slowly rose to her feet, her eyes fixed on the doorway as she rounded the foot of the bed.

Then she saw *it*.

A vapor floated into her room like a billowing puff of smoke. She closed her eyes.

No, this isn't real.

She violently shook her head before opening her eyes.

The cloudy mist remained. As it hovered, its smoky spirals began to take the form of a woman, moving closer and wrapping her in the haze.

"Who are you?" Grace kept the gun pointed at the mist.

"You know who I am. It's *Lillian*."

Grace backed away, bumping into the foot of the bed and falling onto the soft mattress. She allowed the pistol to fall from her fingers and squinted at the lucid vision before her. As the image came into focus, Lillian's golden hair framed her perfect opaque features like a halo. Her green eyes peered expressively at Grace, while her white dress glided and swished around her formless body.

"You're dead. Gone. I don't understand..." Her voice trailed off as her jaw fell open.

"I need your help, Grace."

Her body felt rigid and heavy as if she were glued to the bed. "No, no, this can't be happening. I hate you. You stole William."

"I'm trapped, and I need your help."

Grace gulped, willing herself to move. She had never believed in apparitions, and despite Lillian's ghostly pleas for help, she wasn't about to start now.

"Get out of my house," she hissed, swinging her feet off the bed. "Go someplace where you're wanted. Haunt your *husband*."

"I can't. Your house is positioned along a crux in the ley-lines—a small intersection point linking your world to mine. The others don't know about this gateway, I only found it because I was looking. Please—I'm stuck, and I need your help."

She stood up, saddled her hips with her hands, and cocked her head to one side.

"I can't help you. Leave me alone."

Lillian's eyes danced like luminous emeralds.

"Grace, please. Your hatred of me is fueling the psychic link, please use it to help me. I can't move on to heaven. All the souls are trapped. The Blood Pearl Amulet has been stolen. Without it, the dead cannot pass through the gateway to the great beyond."

Grace lifted her brows. "Amulet? What are you talking about?"

"The amulet is the sacred stone which succeeds in attaining balance between realms. When we die, we pass into a transitional dimension before moving to our final destination. The Blood Pearl Amulet keeps the invisible barrier between Earth and the transitional world intact while acting as the gateway for souls to enter heaven or hell. With the amulet gone, the veil between Earth and the transitional realm will dissolve in twenty-four hours. Your entire world is in great danger! I need you to find the amulet so the balance can be restored and we can move on, or the entities trapped between worlds will spill back into yours, unleashing all kinds of malevolent forces."

Grace frowned. "I don't know... this all sounds pretty farfetched to me. I mean amulets, gateways, and realms?" She clutched a fistful of hair around her temples and shook her head. "I think I'm losing my mind.""

She turned away from Lillian's pleading stare until she felt the frigid sensation on her arm from Lillian's touch.

"Grace, I'm dead, remember? Yet, here you are talking to me as if I were still in your world. You're not losing your mind, I'm as real as I ever was. There will be three cosmic signs confirming my words. The first is a blood moon tonight. A blue moon will follow, marking six hours until the portal opens."

Grace flinched and yanked her arm away. "And the third?"

Lillian lowered her voice. "The invisible barrier between Earth and the transitional sphere will diffuse altogether with a solar eclipse... then your world will flood with ghosts and demon entities. If that happens, it will be too late."

"Blood moons occur every six months—not a rare thing. Blue moons and solar eclipses are not rare either. Sounds pretty flimsy to me."

"Perhaps, but when have these events occurred within a single day?"

Lillian glanced over her shoulder to a dimension invisible to Grace. When she turned back, her eyes were wide and quivering. "I, I have to go. The other souls are coming! Don't be afraid of the dark, Grace." Her hazy image began to dissolve, shrouding over the room before totally disappearing.

Grace's shoulders slumped with her relief. She began a fast pace about her room. "Why is this happening?" she muttered over and over, until finally her legs gave way and she slumped onto her bed.

Her eyes were as wide as light bulbs as she scanned the ceiling, hoping the crusty paint would provide answers. Trying to gather her thoughts, she decided she would treat her newly acquired challenge like any of her other cases. She leapt to her feet and rushed downstairs to her office.

She fired up her laptop, popped the kettle on for more coffee, and settled in for a session of online research. If it was a Blood Pearl Amulet that kept the Earth safe from bad-ass ghosts, she would have to at least check it out. After all, Lillian said she wasn't losing her mind.

Right?

Grace screwed up her face. "Holy shit, I'm listening to a dead person about my mental health and a threat to the world, no less."

A shudder cascaded down her spine, and she wriggled in her chair. Her practical self wanted to ignore her paranormal experience and pretend like it didn't happen. Yet, she couldn't overlook her highly developed instincts, and right now, she knew something was definitely up—especially since she was now talking to dead people.

She turned her attention to Google, pushing aside the creepy feeling. "Okay, Lillian, let's see what we can find about your Blood Pearl."

Hours later and Grace was no closer to a place to start searching for the amulet than when she had begun. She had come across a brief explanation on some shady-looking sorcery website that mentioned a 'Sacred Temple of Death'– the supposed location of the amulet. Only, she couldn't find the exact whereabouts of the temple listed anywhere online. When she scrolled to the bottom of the sorcery site, she almost fell off her chair when she scanned a group of text that read:

The Blood Pearl Amulet; a stone of mystical energy allowing the dead to pass through light or darkness. Its esoteric qualities also keep intact an all-powerful barrier separating the Earth from the transitional soul realm. The barrier cannot be seen in ordinary human experience, for it vibrates at the next, higher octave.

Beware!

Should the Blood Pearl Amulet ever be removed from the

enshrined position in the Sacred Temple of Death, a series of cosmic signs will entail; a blood moon and a blue moon will occur at the 12th and 6th hour, weakening the barrier for ultimate disintegration. Furthermore, a solar eclipse will mark the final hour and "The Bloed Sunder" will unfold. Darkness will blanket the Earth indefinitely as the soul realm overflows into our world.

It is said, the Gods of Death may be temporarily appeased with a "pragtige opoffering"—a female sacrifice—to remind them of humanity's progressive belief in the guardian of the afterworld.

GRACE RUBBED her eyes and blinked. She was practically seeing double from staring at the computer monitor for so long. She picked up the coffee mug and took a sip. Cold coffee ran down her throat like pasty chalk. She scowled and cursed at the mug as she pushed it aside. This was all getting to be too much. Her head throbbed, and her heart banged like crazy against her ribcage as she thought about the Blood Pearl Amulet.

Why is it always a female the gods want for a sacrifice?

Given the dire circumstances, she decided she was going to need some help figuring out this mess before she really did lose her mind. Unfortunately, the few friends she had wouldn't believe this story enough to give up their time searching for a mystical stone.

She jumped to her feet and began to pace around her office as she racked her brain. She might have a shot at convincing one person only to help her—William. She knew his interests included religious history, omens, and voodoo practices among other, unearthly subjects. Not to mention, his wife had initiated this chaos to begin with.

As she reached for her phone to call him, she wandered toward the window and pushed aside the drapes. While the dial tone drilled unanswered in her ear, she admired the deepening blue sky and the first stars beginning to smatter across the horizon. The call rang out. She frowned as she peered at the screen and sent him a quick text message before tucking her phone into her pocket.

He's probably still sleeping off the Valium, she thought.

She lifted her head. Her eyes widened as she gasped, holding a trembling hand over her heart while her body shuddered violently.

All at once, the moon dimmed until it bled, casting an incandescent red glow over the surrounding stars. It was the first sign, just as Lillian and that spooky online website had predicted. And it felt as if she were swallowed whole by the reality of it.

Six a.m. Early, she knew.

"William, let me in," called Grace, pounding on the door.

"Go away," he grumbled from the other side.

She knocked louder. "I need your help, please, William. Let me in."

Silence.

"I am going to keep knocking until you open the door. At least, hear me out."

The door opened a crack and he pressed his eye into it. "What do you want?"

She pushed on the door until he stepped back, then, yanking his arm, she pulled him out onto the porch.

"Hey! What the hell?" he snapped. He snatched his arm away and glared at her. "Grace–"

"Shhh! Wait for it," she said, cutting him short and clasping his wrist again. Her head cranked toward the sky as she scanned the orange hues lighting the horizon. Her eyes flitted toward the still-visible moon and she held her breath.

William tried to release her grip, but her nails clenched in harder.

"Ouch! Grace! What the hell is wrong with—"

"There!" she yelled, tearing him closer as she pointed toward the moon. "It's blue. William—the second sign! Oh my God, oh my God!"

Stepping back, he rubbed the stubble on his chin and frowned as he regarded her. "So what? A blue moon. I'm riveted, Grace. Thanks for waking me up at stupid-o-clock to see this. I'm going back to bed."

He turned to go back inside.

"Wait, what? Didn't you get my message last night? I tried calling you so many times."

He paused and faced her. "Yeah, like six many times."

Grace smiled as she noticed the wild strands of straight thick hair fluffing and jutting on the top of his crown like an adorable puppy.

"I'm sorry about that, were you sleeping?"

He shook his head. "I was out all day yesterday, had to take care of something important—it took a while. *Then* I was sleeping."

Her brows lifted. "Okay then... Well, I know you're going through a lot, but if you read my message about this mystical object thing that went missing, then you'll know I need your help. I have no one else to ask and you know about this kind of stuff."

He looked at her, shaking his head. "Now? What exactly

are you searching for? Your message was like a cryptic puzzle. I was too exhausted to even try and figure it out."

Grace glanced over her shoulder before leaning closer to him. She lowered her voice to a confidential tone.

"It's called a Blood Pearl Amulet. It's supposed to keep our world safe from horrible spirits and keep the balance between realms. It acts as a gateway for the dead to pass through to heaven or hell while protecting the Earth so they don't hang around and torment us, or something..."

His black bushy brows creased. "And? What's this got to do with you? And what's with the hush-hush shit?"

She cleared her throat and straightened up. "Hello? Have you not listened to anything I said? It's missing, William. Someone's taken the amulet from the Sacred Temple of Death, and we need to find it before the world darkens with malicious entities."

He was silent as he regarded her with a scowl firmly implanted upon his features.

She tapped her foot before sighing. "William? Time is ticking—will you help me save the world today or what?"

He held up a palm with a frown. "Thinking. What's up with your hair anyway... and your outfit?" he asked, eyeing her breasts.

She glanced down, noticing she had misbuttoned her blouse. The material gaped opened, revealing the edge of her lacy black bra. She blushed as her fingers fidgeted about adjusting the buttons.

"Given the circumstances, I didn't get much sleep," she said, smoothing her unbrushed hair. "William, please. Lillian came to me, I really nee–"

"Lillian came to you? When? Why didn't she come to me? She's supposed to come back to me..."

"Geez, I *wish* she had come to you. Something about ley-lines and intersection points... the point is, she's in trouble and needs our help."

His dark eyes narrowed. "What *exactly* did she say? Did she give you a message for me?"

Grace took a breath and suppressed a sigh. "I'll tell you everything on the way."

"On the way where?"

"That's what you're gonna tell me. Hurry! Go wash up, your hands are filthy. What have you been doing anyway? Looks like you've been climbing through a cave!"

He knotted his fingers together and gave her a sideways glance as he turned. "I won't be long," he said, then disappeared into the house.

SHE FELT William's eyes on her, his face wrinkled with suspicion.

"Did she really come to you, Grace?"

"Yes."

"How was she? What did she say?"

She threw him a glance. "Well, she was pretty upset. She's stuck in the in-between realm, you know, the transitional world I told you about between Earth and the beyond."

He gazed out the window. "So then, she's still around?"

"Around enough to talk to me. Where are we going, William?"

"Let's try St. Louis Cathedral. Given we are talking about life-and-death issues, they might know something. What do you think?"

Grace nodded. It was as good a place as any to start—

spirits and spiritual entities wouldn't be all that unusual at a church.

As they approached the oldest cathedral in North America, she marveled at its graceful beauty. St. Louis Cathedral sat on the edge of Jackson Square, a bustling tourist destination with street performers, musicians, and pickpockets.

No sooner had they walked through the church doors, they were ushered out with a flurry of commotion. Turned out, the church not only couldn't provide information about the Blood Pearl Amulet and its function in the Sacred Temple of Death, but they also believed their questions to be of a wicked nature and contradictory to their beliefs.

"Well, that went well," said Grace, scowling toward the church doors as they hit the sidewalk. "Now, what?"

William shrugged and concealed his swollen eyes with dark sunglasses. "I need coffee."

"Coffee? Now?" Actually, it wasn't a bad idea. It would help her think. "Okay, then. We'll get some to go."

As they set off toward a nearby cafe, her brain boggled against her skull. She rubbed at her temples as she felt the beginnings of a headache set in.

"Gracie, do you think she'll come to me, too?" William asked as they snaked through the crowd.

"I don't know. I'm as clueless as you. If the Blood Pearl Amulet isn't replaced, I'm not sure what will happen to her. And you know we're probably all going to die, right?"

William gulped. "Die? Listen, Grace, I believe you need to find the Blood Pearl, but don't you think you're being just a little dramatic?"

She halted and glared at him. "Are you fucking serious? Do you really think I'm doing this for my health? I don't know about you, but I don't even want to take the chance the Blood Pearl Amulet is hocus-pocus. I—"

She stopped short as she noticed a gypsy closing in on them, a striking woman with dark, glossy hair almost to her feet, and a neck swathed with jewels that dangled over a vibrant, lilac dress. As she approached them, the gypsy pulled Grace aside, shoved a card into her palm, and whispered, "*The Bloed Sunder.*"

Grace looked at the card.

Voodoo Priestess Ayizan
The Spiritual Temple
5057 North Rampart Street

WHEN SHE LOOKED UP AGAIN, the gypsy woman was gone.

———

THE SILENCE WAS thick as Grace and William drove to the Voodoo Priestess Spiritual Temple on North Rampart Street. Grace's mind was a clutter of possibilities as she mulled over her task of locating the amulet. Unfamiliar words jumbled through her head like a broken puzzle.

Soul realm. Entities. Blood Pearl. And why the hell is this falling into my lap, anyway?

When they entered the shop, the smoke curl of spicy incense burning on an altar made her eyes water. Shelves brimmed with protection oils, healing tonics, love potions, and voodoo dolls. Masks and mysterious sculptures littered the walls, while dream catchers and wind chimes dangled from the ceiling.

An elderly woman of color fiddled about with cards and

books in the back of the temple. Her head and shoulders were draped with a thin silken scarf that fell forward as she leaned toward the shelves. Silver rings adorned her crooked fingers and shined against her dark skin.

William kept his sunglasses on and lingered by the door while Grace cleared her throat as she approached the woman.

"Excuse me. Is Priestess Ayizan here?"

The woman paused, a wide smile slowly spreading across her face. "I am Priestess Ayizan. How can I help you?"

Grace smiled back before looking at the tops of her shoes. "I am looking for an amulet that is extremely powerful. Do you have amulets here?"

"We do, but they are mere trinkets. Can you tell me more about this special amulet or its powers?"

Grace shrugged. "I'm afraid I can only tell you it is blood red and powerful."

The priestess sighed and then her brown eyes widened and she stifled a gasp. "I... I can't help you. You need the witch doctor, *Sangomas*."

"A witch doctor?"

Priestess Ayizan pursed her lips. She nodded gravely. "Come."

She clutched her lower back, making soft grunting sounds as she walked toward the table. She took a pen and scratched on a piece of paper before handing it to her. Her eyes darkened.

"You will find him here. Have there been signs, child?"

Grace swallowed the lump in her throat and nodded. She glanced at William, who was still by the front of the shop looking at a candle display.

"Y-yes," she muttered.

"Then you don't have much time. Legend has it, if the

amulet is removed, spirits both good and bad become trapped in the soul realm and the invisible barrier protecting Earth will disinegrate in twenty-four hours, thus allowing them to invade our world through an open portal. You have been chosen and the well-being of the world rests with you."

Chosen? For what? Grace thought.

Grace clutched the piece of paper. "Thank you, priestess," she said, hurrying from the temple.

"Child! Child!" the priestess called after her.

Grace paused in the doorway, whirling around to look at her.

The elderly woman spoke in a low murmur. "Don't be afraid of the dark."

The words echoed through her mind as Grace ran to the car. William ran after her.

"Grace, come on. You can't really believe in all this 'end of the world' bullshit."

"Really, William? I don't think you're processing things properly right now."

Ah, there's the car.

She looped around the trunk and beeped the locks, starting the engine before his behind reached the seat.

He shot her an exasperated look. "Geez, what's the rush?"

Pulling the car from the curb, she cursed under her breath at a passing cyclist.

"You're definitely out of whack. Didn't you hear the woman? The well-being of the world rests with me. I'm the 'chosen one,' whatever that means. I mean, I think that's a good reason to be in a rush, don't you think, William?"

He was speechless.

GRACE COULD FEEL him shooting daggers at her with his eyes. She exited the interstate, leaving most of the traffic behind as the road became narrow, winding along the flat marshlands as they entered the bayou swamps.

She glanced at the GPS, the computerized voice announcing that they were only minutes from the witch doctor's place. Grace let out an exasperated sigh.

"What? If you have something to say, now is the time to do so."

William shook his head. "I'm just surprised, is all. You were always the practical type. I'd never in a million years think you'd be on some wild voodoo-magic goose chase."

"Yeah, well, things change. Maybe you don't know me as well as you thought. Besides, I think we're past the 'wild goose chase' part—this shit is real."

William turned his head to look at the unending rows of thick cypress trees bordering the water. "Not for me. She came to you, not me, remember." He swung his eyes back to her. "This could be dangerous. We don't know these people. And if anything happened, no one would hear a damn thing."

Grace felt the angry fire burning her throat, her temples throbbing.

This was his *wife. How dare he?*

"I'd rather be sipping a margarita at the fucking Waldorf Astoria with Gerard Butler than driving to a voodoo witch doctor's shack in the god-forsaken swamps. But hey, we don't always get what we want, now do we, William?"

Slowing the car according to the GPS's directions, she turned onto what seemed to be nothing but a muddy trail. Long blades of grass brushed against the windows. The car dipped and bumped along, frightening a flock of heron from the underbrush and into the clearing ahead.

Grace pulled to a stop before a dilapidated, stilted house perched along the banks of the marsh.

"This is it," she said, gathering her bag and getting out of the car.

She took a few strides before glancing back at the car. William hadn't moved. Muttering under her breath, she retraced her steps and opened the car door.

"We don't have all day. In fact," she fumbled in her bag and pulled out her cell before looking back at him. "We have less than three hours to find this Blood Pearl Amulet before we all become ghost bait. Are you coming with me or not?"

He rubbed the bristles on his chin and studied the house. Grotesque black masks hung along the grimy outside walls. Some had been painted and jeweled, others were trimmed with straw-like beards, rows of teeth glimmering between the dark wood. He shuddered.

"Are you sure about this?"

She reached for his arm and yanked hard. "Oh, for God's sake!"

William stood two steps behind Grace as she knocked on the door. She held her breath as she heard footsteps approaching from the other side of the door.

Silence.

Don't be afraid of the dark.

"Grace?" William whispered behind her.

"Hmm?"

"I don't want to be ghost bait. I, I have to tell you something."

She shot him a look. "Now?"

She hissed, startling when she heard the door handle begin to twist.

White paint flaked to the floor as the door opened. Grace gasped as the witch doctor's massive frame filled the doorway. The African-American man stared down at her, his eyes bulging and his teeth gleaming beneath the curl of his lips. The buttons of his brown-smeared shirt strained against his wide girth while he grumbled beneath his breath and scrutinized them.

"You!" His voice shook the air like a summer thunderstorm. He raised a long, bony finger and pointed it at Grace.

She froze. "Me?"

"Yes. You must be the one seeking the lost Blood Pearl. You are the *chosen one*. I see the vision now. Come, hurry. We don't have much time," he said, ushering them inside.

As they entered the house, the first thing Grace noticed was the chaotic muddle filling the room. Puffs of white furniture filling poked in all directions from the floral-covered chairs, while the area was bountiful with stacks of books, boxes, and rolled-up rugs. A thick layer of dust crusted over the tables and television, while yellow frayed curtains were loosely drawn across the windows. Burning incense fused with the scent of freshly brewed tea and wafted through the hazy room, yet it didn't disguise the putrid stench firmly ingrained within the furniture.

She screwed up her face toward William and shrugged as the witch doctor pushed them each into a chair.

"About the Blood Pearl, that's why we're here. I—"

The witch doctor's voice boomed over her. "Yes! But wait! I am *Sangomas* and it is customary to offer my guests tea to honor the world of the dead." He paused, eyeing her with a peculiar grin. "Especially one of your status."

She shot William a look. He gave her a wide-eyed shrug.

"What are you talking about?" she said, swinging her gaze back to the witch doctor.

The floorboards groaned as the big man jittered on his feet. "You—the chosen one!"

"Thank you, but we don't have time for tea. If we could just get back to the Blood Pearl Amulet-"

He raised a flat palm in the air, his voice drowning out hers. "First, we have tea. I insist on behalf of the gods."

She clamped her jaw shut and nodded silently.

He grinned and whirled about, disappearing through an open doorway and clanking around in the kitchen. She gazed around at the clutter of shelves laden with hand-blown glass bottles filled with potions, jars containing grotesque animal parts suspended in liquid, voodoo dolls, pendulums, iron cauldrons, and candles.

She almost jumped from her chair when William's voice cut through her thoughts.

"Gracie, we need to talk. Let's go outside."

"Just hold on a sec," she whispered back, twirling her eyes to the witch doctor as he returned from the kitchen.

"Here. Drink."

The witch doctor grinned, handing them each a goblet filled with hot tea.

She sipped on the sweet, warm liquid, her empty stomach growling as she drank the milky black tea. It tasted like lemon and honey, and it was the best thing she'd had all day. She gulped at the hot brew.

The witch doctor watched them. "It's good, yes?"

"Yes, thank you," Grace said, setting her empty goblet on the chipped timber coffee table before her. "Now, about the amulet, we were given information leading us here in hope you might help us find it?"

The man leaned back in his chair. "I am *Sangomas*,

guardian of the Sacred Temple of Death. It is of vital impor-
tance to attain a balanced reconciliation between the world
of the living and the world of the dead. The Blood Pearl
provides a continuity between life and death, allowing souls
to experience the transition in peace."

He paused, and his eyes seemed to darken.

"The Blood Pearl Amulet has been removed from its
sacred position. When the hour falls dark with the solar
eclipse, so, too, will the portal to Earth open, unleashing a
parade of entities, the like of which you've never imagined
in your wildest nightmares. That hour is called, *The Bloed
Sunder*."

"Holy shit," William said. "It's all true."

Grace's head began to throb, an incessant thumping
blossomed in pain from behind her eyes. She lifted her
hands to rub her temples, yet, she couldn't feel her fingers. A
heaviness began to creep into her entire body, her eyelids
drooping.

What's going on?

"Luckily, you've come to *me*," he said, grinning and
leaning closer to her face. "A sacrifice will appease the
gods of death until the next blood moon, giving me more
time to find the Blood Pearl Amulet. Your death will keep
the invisible barrier to the soul realm intact. The *chosen
one* always reveals herself in the final hours before *The
Bloed Sunder*, thus showing the Gods of Death our
continued faith in the guardian of the afterworld and the
cycle of life and death. You will save the world, *pragtige
opoffering*."

"Me?" She spat the word, her tongue feeling as though it
had been wrapped in cotton. "What did you... Give us?"

"*Slaap doepa!*"

The witch doctor threw his head back and laughed, a

142

roaring cackle that felt like a railroad spike through her temples.

Grace felt as though fire pulsed through her veins.

No!

She fought to keep her head up, turning to look at William. His dark hair fell over his eyes, his face pale as milk as he slumped in his chair, the silver goblet falling to the floor.

William! William!

Her head began to spin, her vision blackening from the edges.

Don't be afraid of the dark.

LILLIAN HOVERED ABOVE WILLIAM. A feeling of helplessness weighed her down as she watched his still body. He hadn't moved since the witch doctor had dragged Grace from the room. Strands of hair stuck against his forehead, clinging over his eyes and concealing most of his face as he hunched forward in the oversized chair.

She knew he hadn't died because she hadn't felt his essence crossing over. Yet, she knew this could be her only chance to reach him before it was too late. A flash of guilt pulsed through her being. Grace and William had been put in this predicament because of her. It would be up to her to make things right.

She gazed at William again. Perhaps it would be better to forsake them now, rather than deal with what they would face if the portal opened. Lillian turned from him, floating toward the grimy ceiling, trying not to look back at the man she loved.

Voices. They whispered to her, the voice of every broken

heart, crying out from the soul realm as they had been denied their final resting place.

Lillian stopped. She knew what had to be done. If the Blood Pearl Amulet wasn't found, this would become every soul's fate.

She whirled around to look at William. If she didn't do something, he, too, would remain with the fallen in a realm between the promised land and a blazing abyss.

Her being vibrated along the waning soul realm barrier. The time was drawing closer, causing miniscule fissures to appear around the fringes of the invisible boundary.

There must be a way to reach him.

Her thoughts scattered like rolling dice until she realized a different way—a higher, divine power surrounding all of creation way. If she could just align herself with that source energy, she might have a chance of reaching him.

She staked her intention firmly into her consciousness, and focused her attention on his motionless body. She felt a tranquil energy begin to envelop her. As it gained momentum, she thrived with the thread of empowerment laced within its mystical fibers. The feeling took hold deep within her being, smothering her like a glowing cocoon until the divine strength invaded part of her soul.

Her world narrowed over him and as she had been set into motion, her being pushed through the barrier and spilled into the room next to his slumbering body. She stood over him, cloaking him with her presence, bathing his soul with the devotion of her own. She smiled, her green eyes reaching the deepest recess of his being as he awakened.

His long lashes blinked up at her. "Lillian. What? How?"

She stroked his face with her hand, smoothing his frown.

"Oh, William!" she cried, falling into his arms.

His overjoyed heart tumbled into hers as they came together in a moment of recklessness. A current of tenderness flourished between them as they basked under a radiant light blooming in every direction, the light of all creation.

His eyes crinkled. "Have you come back to me?"

"My love, I'm sorry I left you so suddenly, but this is not the way—you need to let me go now."

She sent her mental energies to him, silently communicating all the words she had collected since her passing. Unspoken words that had gathered on the tip of her tongue and stung her heart every time she watched him grieve her death. They poured from her soul like an overflowing river, rippling through his awareness and lifting his consciousness with a gentle wave of love.

Her eyes penetrated his being. She showed him the chaotic soul realm, and the evil entities pressing and throbbing against the invisible barriers that would break when the solar eclipse darkened the Earth. She revealed to him the suffering and despair at the turn of *The Bloed Sunder*.

In turn, all his deepest secrets were revealed to her as he bared his soul, confessing the actions that ultimately brought them together at this hour.

She pulled away from him, searching his eyes, eager to receive his understanding.

"I will always love you," she said.

Tears cascaded over his face, he wiped at them with balled fists as he nodded. "I know. Take my love with you and keep it safe until I see you again."

She smiled and clasped a hand over her heart. "It is deep within me, in every form I take."

A sob caught in his throat. "I just needed to see you again. And you came to me..."

She felt the pull. She understood. Her time with him had come to an end.

"It's time. We must both go."

He reached for her as she floated away, his fingers swiping at the air while she faded from the room.

"I love you, Lillian. I'm sorry."

———

GRACE SHOOK HER HEAD—HER eyes shot open. The rank odor of mold and incense filled her nostrils, her world blackened by the mask cloaking her face. She tried to move, but thick ropes cut into her wrists and ankles. Her heart thumped against her ribcage with the race of her pulse. Grace gasped and choked beneath the mask, swinging her head in attempt to dislodge it.

"Ah, there you are, my *pragtige opoffering*."

She wanted to scream, but the lump in her throat wouldn't allow it. Her eyes blinked wildly, desperate to know her whereabouts.

Where is William?

Her mind raced with possibilities—all of them dark, and threatening to paralyze her.

Don't be afraid of the dark.

She struggled to breathe.

"Come, come. Let me help you." The witch doctor's thick voice curled through her mask and twisted in her ears.

She shrank back as his thick fingers crawled over her like a deadly spider. Suddenly, air and light rushed in as the witch doctor yanked the suffocating mask from her head. She blinked, gasping as his image floated in her fuzzy vision.

He wore nothing but a flimsy swath of fabric over his

groin and a hideous black mask with big, painted teeth and long, golden straw sprouted from the edges, spilling over his shoulders. The witch doctor's dark, oiled skin reflected the flames that reached almost to the roof behind him.

As her vision cleared, Grace thought they were in a cave. Her eyes darted about, looking at hanging strands of colored beads and bells, rattles made from bone, candles, and amulets. A ring of sacred stones rimmed the fire pit, while knives, blades, and bottles of rum adorned a table.

"Welcome to the Temple of Death. You've awakened just in time, *pragtige opoffering*."

His voice sounded surly and muffled from behind the mask. He spun around on his heels, lunging at the table where a collection of blades sat. He reached for a long-bladed knife, whistling as he tossed the handle from palm to palm before turning his head in her direction.

As he approached, Grace gulped and turned her trembling chin away from him, the blade of his knife dancing in the flaring fire. His hot breath brushed past her ear as he leaned close.

"It is time, *pragtige opoffering*," he said, raising the blade. "I'm going to split you from ear to ear. You'll hardly feel a thing."

The witch doctor backed away, slipping the mask to the top of his head and grinning at her. His throat vibrated as an eerie, low chant reverberated through the cave while his body gyrated according to the ritual.

Grace shuddered. Her eyes were glued to him, thoughts rushing though her mind like a tornado. She strained against the knots at her wrists, feeling her own blood on her skin. Her ears filled with the churn of restless spirits, curdling groans drumming in her head as they started to break through the invisible soul realm barrier. She tore her eyes from the witch doctor, a silent gasp catching in her throat when she caught sight of a thousand faceless images pulsating and twisting against the cave walls and ceiling. They scratched and clawed excitedly with each beat of the witch doctor's mantra until the grisly hymns morphed into a single, chilling phrase.

The Bloed Sunder.

Lifting his arms high, the witch doctor let loose a high-pitched call while waving his hands in the air. His intonations rose and fell. He closed in on her with the knife, rapidly shortening the gap between them.

Grace closed her eyes. Tears streaked her face, her chest heaving uncontrollably.

"Stop!"

William's voice boomed through the cave with the force of a blasting cannonball.

She gasped. Grace looked at William. He stood next to the fire with his arm outstretched, holding an amulet. As it dangled from his hand, she noticed the polished shock of red stone within its golden encasing. The Blood Pearl.

The witch doctor stopped and then spun around to face William.

"I have the Blood Pearl Amulet!" William thrust the amulet toward the witch doctor.

Silence fell upon the cave.

The witch doctor's head fell to one side. "Ah, yes. It was you I chased through the marsh yesterday, thief," he said, his voice thick with venom. He gave a low cackle. "You are very fast, but perhaps not so smart about returning to the scene of your crime."

A rumbling growl came from deep within the fire, and the witch doctor flew at him, running into William and tackling him to the ground. The knife toppled from his hand

and clanked against the stone as his massive fists slammed into William's head.

Grace shifted, ignoring the increasing pain in her ankles and wrists. "No! William!"

The witch doctor sprang to his feet, grabbed the knife, and charged toward her. His dark eyes were glazed with lunacy.

"You are the *pragtige opoffering*," he said, bringing the blade to her throat. "The ceremony must go on! The gods will have you before the amulet!"

Grace turned her head and braced herself for the blade.

The cut never came. Instead, a bloodcurdling scream preceded a heavy thud as William hit the witch doctor with a heavy, brass candelabra in the back of his head.

Grace watched the witch doctor fall unconscious to the ground as William ran over and began to cut her free.

She fell into his arms, sobbing against his chest.

"I'm so sorry, Gracie. I'm so sorry." He coughed and spoke through silent tears. "It was me. I stole the Blood Pearl."

She gazed up at him. "Why?"

He looked away from her. "The voodoo priestess—she told me about the amulet. I was desperate to get Lillian back. I didn't listen to her warnings. I just wanted her back."

"William," her voice broke. She lifted her head and looked around. "Do you hear that?"

"What?"

"The ghosts and demons. I can hear them. They're almost here," she whispered, her eyes darting around the cave.

She screeched hysterically, gripping William's arm as she saw monstrous features become clearer along the stone walls. Black hollow eyes stared down at her while razor-sharp teeth gnawed against the invisible boundary, their opened mouths contorting with their repugnant song.

"We need to return the amulet, William. Now!"

The golden flames raged around the altar. William used a bucket full of water to dampen the fire long enough for Grace to climb into the blistering ring of heat. She stood looking down at the altar, her brow clustered with sweat while she scanned the intrinsic weave of channels carved within the brass shrine. Jewels and stones crusted along an engraved spiralling symbol, and she traced the grooves with a hovering finger until reaching the center of the wreath. Within the ornamental braid, she noticed an impression. Her mind raced as the eerie phantom chants pressed urgently in her ears as she raised the amulet in her trembling hand and studied it for a moment. The cavity was a perfect match to the Blood Pearl Amulet.

There she stood, silently giving thanks and blessings to the continuity between life and death before locking the amulet into its sacred position.

The flames immediately died and a radiant light streamed over the temple. Orbs appeared like bubbles of light, floating around Grace and William.

Grace silently gazed around the cave, her body quaking with relief as tears streamed from her eyes. She looked at William. He was watching her steadily, his own eyes mirroring hers.

He smiled. "You did it, Gracie. You saved the world today. You *are* the chosen one."

She stepped away from the altar, her respite dissolving as she approached him.

"What the hell were you thinking? You almost got me killed," she said, slugging him in the arm.

He reeled backward, groping at his arm before lowering his chin and giving her a droopy stare.

"I deserved that—and more. I'm sorry. I haven't been thinking straight since Lillian's death. If I knew this was going to happen..."

He stopped short when, from one of the bubbles, an image appeared. Lillian smiled down at them and waved, her green eyes sparkling like a vivid green ocean.

"Goodbye, my love," she said to William, her voice ringing like a glorious musical note before she ascended, taking the light-bubble with her.

He waved at her receding image. "Goodbye, Lillian. I'll love you forever."

Grace saw tears of joy on William's face as he bid his wife a final farewell.

"What now?"

"Now, we get the hell out of here."

He pulled her hand gently into his.

"Come on, Gracie," he said, leading her from the cave.

She knotted her fingers through his while sticking as close to him as possible.

I am not afraid of the dark.

ABOUT THE AUTHORS

Kim Petersen

Kim Petersen is an award-winning urban fantasy author of the Millie's Angel series. She lives along the rugged shore lines of the Australian east coast with her tribe, and loves to write with the ocean. Kim loves hanging out with her family, and is happiest when crafting tales that delve into the minds of beautifully twisted characters that ponder the secrets of life and death.

Discover more about Kim: www.kimpetersen.com.au

Shirley Hartnett

I'm an Indie Mystery Author who absolutely loves to write. I have an extensive background in math and physics so I always stir that into any story. I'm also doing Science Fiction and fantasy. I've got plenty of stories to come out soon, please keep an eye out for new releases!

Find out more at http://www.shartnettwrites.com

BLOOD MAGIC

BY JILL HARRIS and Caroline Hanson

EMMA MACKENZIE STEPPED out of the taxi into a sultry late afternoon in Louisiana, wishing she'd managed to sleep on the plane. The strains of a jazz trumpet blasted out the open doors of a restaurant down the street, and the smell of fried seafood caught in her throat.

An elderly man in cut-off jeans wandered up to her. His face was so lined it looked as if someone had raked his skin with sharp fingernails. He smelled strongly of alcohol and was talking loudly to himself. She clutched her suitcase tighter, wondering if she might need to make a break for it or use it as a weapon.

He glared at Emma for a moment with wide, bloodshot eyes. Then he laughed. A low, mean sound. A group of tourists jostled past on the sidewalk and the drunkard melted into the crowd. She hadn't realized New Orleans would be so threatening, and so quickly.

Despite the heat, a shiver passed through her as she

dragged her suitcase to the wrought-iron gates of the house on Bourbon Street that she'd inherited from her deceased great-aunt. The three-story, red-brick, flat-fronted house had green shutters on all except the top-floor windows. A balcony with metal railings ran the length of the second floor, and like many houses in the French Quarter, it had seen better days.

Emma unlocked the gate. Rust flaked off the brass handle as she turned it. The main door was at the side of the building down a cool, narrow alleyway full of shadows.

The gate clanged shut behind her.

A few steps into the murk took her to the green door, paint peeling and cracking away from the pale wood underneath. It was the sort of door one saw in a horror movie, she thought grimly. Keeping with this morbid idea, it looked as though someone had scratched a word on the left side of the lock with a knife. Emma peered at it, but time had left it illegible except for the first letter.

B.

Entering the house, she threw down her bag on one of the many chairs in the hallway and stepped over piles of books, ornately carved statues and beads on her way back down the dim corridor leading from the back of the house to the side door. She hadn't been in the house for more than five minutes before there was a loud knocking.

Emma stopped dead. How had someone gotten into the alley down the side? Then she realized—she'd forgotten to lock the gate.

There wasn't a peephole and considering New Orleans was notoriously dangerous (at least that's what her mother told her—but the woman was afraid of everything from a bit of rain to small dogs), the lack of a peephole seemed like a bit of an oversight.

Standing on the doorstep was not only the handsomest man Emma had ever seen. He was taller than average, and the moment she opened the door, he removed his black sunglasses.

His eyes were a pale brown that almost seemed to glow. She blinked and looked again. His eyes were normal, not shining like she'd initially thought. Maybe it was contacts. Like those people who got fake cat eyes or wanted their eyes to look blue instead of dark brown.

And he did seem a bit eccentric. He was dressed in a suit, expensive material, light gray. Like a businessman on lunch. Despite the heat of the day and the blue, cloudless sky, he carried an umbrella. He held it like a parasol, shielding himself from even the faintest hint of the sun.

"Can I help you?" she asked. She tried to peer around him at the gate, but his umbrella made it impossible to tell.

His smile was wide. His teeth even and straight. "I'm Robert. Robert Lyon from Landow and Smith Homes."

She waited. His smile didn't budge. "I'm a real estate agent. I was hoping you might let me take a look around the property."

"Why would I do that?" she asked, because it seemed like a famously bad idea to let a stranger with a manly parasol into the house. "Were you watching me?"

He looked a bit surprised. "Watching you? No. Why? I don't even know your name."

"I'm Emma Mackenzie, and this is my great aunt's home. I just got here. That's all."

"Lucky coincidence, I suppose," he said. His gaze met hers and she blushed, a warmth stealing through her.

Which was ridiculous.

"I spoke to Dorothy? The previous occupant. She was

thinking of selling the home. We had an appointment today."

"She was?" Emma asked. This was news to her. And what did it mean that Dorothy had been about to sell the place and then, she'd died? Had she somehow known, on some subconscious level, that she wasn't well?

"Indeed, she was," he said.

Emma thought she caught the faintest hint of a lilt to his words. French, maybe? Although he sounded American enough, as far as she could tell. His vowels had that soft roundness she always heard on TV.

He leaned a little closer, just a touch, his voice low. "It's quite punishing out here. How about if you invite me in, just for a quick look around and then, I'll be out of your hair."

There wasn't any harm in it, she supposed. And she did need a real estate agent. Perhaps it should be someone devastatingly handsome who helped her sell the place. It beat the crotchety estate agent in England who'd sold Emma her flat, and had shed cat hair from his tweedy jacket while trailing cigarette smoke wherever he went. Emma backed up, opening the door for him to enter.

"May I come in?" he asked, the words oddly formal.

"Yes, of course," she said, moving aside.

A faint smile. And then, he stepped over the threshold, his umbrella closing with a small click.

***

"YOU REALLY DISLIKE THE SUN, I see? In England, we get so little of it that every opportunity to dash into the sunshine is taken," she said, aware she was on the verge of babbling.

Robert seemed distracted by a painting on the wall of a woman dancing naked around a campfire, her arms raised above her head, holding in her hands an enormous snake. When he turned back to Emma, his smile affected her, rolled through her just like the warm sun he worked so hard to avoid.

"It's because I'm a vampire," he said, his gaze scanning the room, already measuring and pricing, she assumed.

"Funny. You must get sick of all the Anne Rice jokes."

"You have no idea," his voice sounded deep and sincere. "So, that's an interesting painting you got over there," he said, referring to the woman with the snake. It was a fairly crude picture, not the sort of thing one would find in her mother's sitting room back home.

"It's my aunt's. Probably not something worth shipping back over to England."

"It's Maîtresse Brigitte, you know."

"I don't know of her. Who is she?"

Robert gave her a long look. "She's a voodoo spirit. With a special interest in fertility and cemeteries."

"Sex and death. I'm sure Freud would have something to say about that."

His expression was grim. "She's powerful. Maybe Dorothy asked her for something nice."

Emma didn't believe any of that but still, it was creepy. "Are you saying she grants wishes? Like a fairy godmother?"

"That's exactly what I'm saying. But you have to give her what she wants or she'll be your worst nightmare. If she doesn't get payment on time, she doesn't like it."

She led the way into the kitchen and filled the kettle, just to give her hands something to do. She hoped her great-aunt had been a tea drinker.

"So, how soon are you going to get out of here?" Robert asked.

Emma was taken aback. "I don't know. A week or two, I

suppose. I'm not sure what to do with her stuff. She collected a lot of tat, really, nothing worth keeping. I guess I'll have to donate most of it. "

"I know people. I could have a truck here in the morning. Help you clear up. In fact, why don't you let me put you up in a hotel or something? Surely you don't want to stay here? I'd think it would be quite sad, being reminded of her."

"I didn't know her, really. She left the UK over twenty years ago. I met her once, as a little girl, but that was it. The family called her Dotty Dot. She was eccentric, my mother said."

He nodded. "I see. So, you don't know what she was doing when she died."

Something about his tone made Emma uneasy. Opening a cupboard, she was relieved to find a box of herbal tea bags. "She had a heart attack in bed. I don't know what else you mean."

"Oh, nothing," he said, and he turned away from her. "Mind if I have a look around?"

He strode out and Emma went after him into the living room, another embarrassingly untidy room stuffed to the rafters with old furniture, glass lamps, strings of beads and hundreds of black votive candles in an array of holders.

Robert's eyes scanned everywhere, from the ceiling to the floor. He even peered behind furniture. "Why don't I just show myself around a bit? Give you a chance to get your things together."

Talking with him was giving her whiplash. Considering how attractive he was, it was a shame he was so socially awkward. But maybe that was for the best. Daniel was back in England, waiting for her, wanting to get back together. A problem for another time. When she wasn't dealing with a dead aunt's worldly goods and a pushy realtor. Robert's words sunk in. "Why would I get my things?"

"For the hotel, of course," he said, as if it were the most natural thing in the world.

"I'm not going to a hotel."

"You wouldn't have to pay for it, of course. Big house like this is worth quite a bit. I'll take it out of my fee. Just think how much sooner you can get it on the market."

Emma thought about it. Not for long, because she wasn't planning on leaving. Not tonight. And she wasn't even sure he was right. How would it make the process go faster?

"No. Thanks," she said.

But Robert was disappearing, wandering back into the kitchen. She found him there looking in the cupboards. It was weird. And intrusive.

The full reality of her situation began to sink in. What the hell had she been thinking, letting a strange man into the house? She hadn't even had a business card from him. He could be a stalker. A killer.

She scooted closer to the wooden knife block, her eyes focused on him as he opened the pantry and squatted down, looking at the shelves and for some inexplicable reason— the undersides of them all. She couldn't begin to imagine what he thought he was looking for, but she had to admit the man had a mighty fine backside.

Emma rested a hand on the counter, bare inches from the knife block, hoping she looked casual. She had to get him out of here. "I just remembered I have to go somewhere. Why don't you give me your card and we can set up an appointment in a day or two? You can have a good look at the place then. When I've had time to tidy up."

He rose slowly, turning to face her and his gaze shifted

pointedly to the knives, as if he could read her mind. As if he knew she wanted a weapon.

"Perhaps we got off on the wrong foot," he said, reaching into his pocket. He pulled out a card and came closer, holding it out to her, the card pinched between two fingers.

She took the card and gave it a swift glance. Robert Lyon, Landow and Smith Homes Real Estate, she read. It put her a little bit at ease. But not enough.

"This won't take long. Promise. Just five minutes and I'll be on my way," he said. His gaze caught hers, the words searing into her mind. Emma opened her mouth to agree, deciding against her better judgment that there wasn't any good reason for him to not look around. *What was wrong with her?* It was unlike her to be so jittery.

A knock sounded at the door and she tore her eyes away from Robert, jerking her gaze to the right, stepping away from him. When had he moved so close? And why had she almost agreed to let him keep looking around? She wanted him gone.

"Coming," she shouted.

She didn't exactly run to the door, but it wasn't far off.

Emma opened the door without hesitation. Standing there was another handsome man. Blond, this time. Apparently, the neighborhood was crawling with them.

"Can I help you?" she asked.

"I'm Mark. Dorothy was my girlfriend," he said. And his eyes filled with tears.

Emma's mouth gaped open. It was on the tip of her tongue to ask if he'd made a mistake because he was at least forty years younger than her aunt. But he was here. And he did know her name. Plus, he was crying. Sobbing, really. It made her feel like a jerk for being dry-eyed in the face of such grief, but she hadn't known Dorothy. Although she was obviously a woman who enjoyed life to the full, younger men and all.

"I'm so sorry for your loss," Emma managed, gesturing for him to come in. Why not? The place was as busy as King's Cross station, for God's sake.

Mark stepped into the house, rifling around in his pockets and pulling out a well-used tissue. Gross.

"Hang on. Let me get you something for that," she said, and left him there. She went to the bathroom and found Robert in there, poking around. "You know what? Get out. You might be a great agent but I don't see how searching under bathroom cabinets is necessary for appraising the house."

"Please, I just need another minute," he said, his smile forced.

"No. Now. Or I'm going to call the police," she said, standing tall. A flash of pride went through her. That was exactly the sort of thing someone said on *Eastenders* to get troublemakers to leave the pub.

Robert grimaced. "If I told you this house was cursed and I was just trying to keep you safe, would you believe me?"

The nerve of him! And the ridiculousness of his statement. How gullible did he think she was? "No, actually. I wouldn't."

He sighed, running a hand through his dark hair. "That's what I thought you'd say. Right. Fine. You've got my card. Call me if..." he seemed at a loss for words. "Call me if something weird happens."

"Something weird has already happened. My great-aunt is dead and her astonishingly young boyfriend is out in the living room waiting for me to bring him a tissue. Go now," she said.

Robert tilted his head to the side. "Younger, huh?"

"It's like a reverse Mick Jagger. Maybe she left instructions on how to replicate the effect. The juicy crone or whatever. I'll be rich. Now leave," she said.

He threw up his hands. "Fine. I'm going." He glowered at Mark on his way out, but the poor man was so busy blowing his nose, he didn't even notice the agent looking at him. After a few torturous minutes, she managed to get Mark out the door, too. He'd taken a few things with him. His clothes, a toothbrush, a gigantic box of condoms, which was rather astonishing, and a pillow which he said would remind him of Dorothy. She tried to get him to take some more things, but he just started crying and finally left.

EMMA WENT upstairs with her suitcase and after a thorough search, found only one bedroom in a fit state to sleep in. Dorothy's bedroom. It was decorated in a heady mix of witch's cave and French boudoir. The woman must have been fearless and Emma was beginning to regret not knowing her.

She spent a while taking it all in. Walls painted a dark pink, a vintage French farmhouse wooden dressing table covered with bottles of scent, strings of beads and powder compacts. Floaty dresses were draped over chairs. An enormous and neatly made four-poster bed stood in the middle of the room.

She padded across the plush red carpet and sank down on the side of the four-poster. It was strewn with swathes of bright-colored sari fabrics, and smelled of roses. Pillows and cushions had been stacked against the headboard.

Dorothy had died in this bed. Emma shivered.

Someone had lovingly made it and presumably changed the black silk sheets since the undertaker took her body away.

And they'd left a large kitchen knife on the mattress, the handle matching the set in the block by the stove.

Emma found it when she ran her hand over the satin coverlet. Yet she was sure she hadn't spotted it when she first came in. For a moment, she thought of Mark, the distraught boyfriend. On one hand, she didn't think he was weird enough to go wandering around his dead lover's room with a sharp blade.

But who knew? This was New Orleans and they did things differently here.

She swallowed hard, fighting a sense of deep unease. Her last meal had been a salad at London airport, so she made her way downstairs to the kitchen, hoping to find something to eat—when someone knocked on the door. She hoped it wasn't Mark again. The idea of dealing with a sobbing man on an empty stomach was just too much.

"Who is it?" Emma asked, through the door.

"It's Robert. I have pizza," he said.

"Why?"

"Persistence? It's the best pizza in New Orleans."

Her stomach rumbled, making the decision for her. What the hell. Although he was weird, he was cute and truth be told, after the disconcerting knife situation earlier, she really didn't mind some company.

She opened the door and was struck again by how good-looking he was. Full lips, aquiline nose, quick smile—like she imagined an Italian aristocrat would have. He held the pizza before him like an offering, and smiled.

She waved him inside. "What kind is it?" she asked.

"I wasn't sure what you would like. So it's half-vegetarian

and half-combo. I figure you can take off whatever you don't like."

"That's really thoughtful," she said. Because it was. Danny wouldn't have thought to do that. He'd have gotten whatever he liked and assumed she'd be happy. Another mark against getting back together with him, she decided.

They went into the kitchen and she pulled down two plates from the shelf.

"I already ate," he said. "But I'd love a drink."

"Oh. I have no idea what she has."

His smile was roguish. "Well, at the risk of getting thrown out, I'm happy to have a look around and see what I can find."

She chuckled, charmed by his willingness to make fun of himself. "Fine. Have a look around. But I'll bet you ten pounds there isn't anything in her bathroom cupboard."

"Ten pounds? You're in America now, sweetheart. And I reserve the right to take you up on that bet."

It took him five minutes to discover a bottle of Jamaican rum under the sink. He held it up to the light. Floating at the bottom was a rather shriveled red chili. Emma passed on the rum.

She took a bite of the pizza and almost moaned. Packing was hard work. She was working on her second piece when he came back into the room.

"Do you like jazz? I know some fantastic music halls," he said.

She paused, considering his odd language. "Do they call them music halls? I thought they were clubs."

His brow furrowed. "You may be right. I don't go very often. English isn't my first language. Every now and again, I wind up with an outdated word."

"Ah," she said, and took her plate, piled high with pizza, to the dining room table.

He sat opposite her, drinking his drink.

"How long have you been a real estate agent?" she asked.

He was staring down into his glass like the answer to the universe was engraved on the bottom. "Did you know your aunt made this rum and chili for a reason?"

"I don't," she said.

"It's commonly used as a sacred offering to Maîtresse Brigitte."

"You're looking at me like I'm supposed to say something now or do something."

"Between the alcohol and the lovely snake painting, I'm thinking your aunt was practicing voodoo."

She wasn't sure if she should laugh or be insulted. "Isn't it what people do here?"

He grimaced. "Some people do. Not like they used to. But the spirits are strong. Strong enough to harm." His gaze was fixed on hers. "To kill. If your aunt disrespected the spirits—who knows how they might have punished her."

She expected him to laugh or something. But he didn't. "You're serious?"

"I wish I wasn't."

"You believe not only that my aunt was practicing voodoo, but that the magic is real?"

"I don't think it, Emma. I know. Voodoo is dangerous and your aunt was in over her head."

"So... are you trying to tell me you think she was killed by voodoo?"

"I'm afraid so," he said, utterly sincere.

"Damn," she said, and wiped her hands on her napkin. "Here I was thinking I was spending time with a normal, attractive guy and now, you've gone and blown it."

His eyes widened. Surprised by her blunt speaking perhaps. "I'm really jetlagged," she said, standing. "But I'm happy to list the house with you. Bring a contract by tomorrow if you want and I'll sign it."

He didn't stand. "Emma, I mean it. And now, you're here and whatever she was up to, she didn't complete it. The spirits might be angry. And if they are, you're not safe."

She crossed her arms and glared at him. "Is that why you wanted me to stay in a hotel?"

"Yes. It's also why I was rummaging around the house. She must be keeping her altar somewhere. If we can find it, we can make sure it's all right for you to stay here."

"Well, I've looked all over the house and surprise, surprise, I haven't seen an altar, a vat of chicken feet or even a stray feather. I think I'm fine."

"It's not safe," he said, voice soft and earnest.

Suspicion filled her. "You're not really an estate agent, are you?"

He sighed and stood. "No, I'm not. I'm a paranormal investigator."

She tried not to laugh. She failed. "Well, I have your card," she said when she stopped laughing. "If something happens, I know who to call. Except your card is fake as it turns out and these probably aren't your details. Now, I think it's time for you to leave."

"Emma, please. Don't kick me out. What's the harm in humoring me, at least?"

"I have humored you. I heard you out. I ate your pizza and let you into my house. You looked around and so did I. There is no altar." And she led him toward the door.

"I don't want to leave you alone here," he said.

"Well, then, it's a good thing you don't have any control over my actions, isn't it? Because I'm ready for you to leave. Goodbye, Robert," she said, and reached for the doorknob.

But she couldn't touch it. Her hand was stopped, a few inches from the door, by what felt like an invisible wall. It was cold to the touch, sending a shock of ice up her arm. She placed a hand flat along the surface, trying to reach the door.

"What the hell?" she asked.

"At the risk of being deeply obnoxious—I told you so."

Panic and confusion filled her. "I don't understand."

"Your aunt practiced voodoo and she pissed off the spirits and died. Now you're here, and the spirits want appeasement. Or else."

She whirled around. "You're joking."

"Me? I'm not amused."

She went to the window and reached out to open the latch, but again, something stopped her. As if there was some barrier keeping her from leaving.

"What do we do? How do we get out?" she asked, not waiting for an answer as she went around the house, trying to get to any window she could and finding the same invisible barrier in every room.

"You're sure you haven't seen an altar? Some kind of table with a statue, candles, incense. Lots of candles. Maybe an animal skull."

She practically growled at him. "I think I'd remember it if I'd seen any such thing. I'm calling the police."

"I don't think they'll be able to help."

She went to grab her phone from her bag. "I've got no reception," she said as the full horror of the situation became clear. They were trapped here. For how long? And by what? A supernatural voodoo entity? It was unbelievable. Impossible.

Alas, a more sensible, reasonable explanation didn't come to her.

A sense of panic buzzed in her stomach.

"You have to get me out of here," she said. Her heart was beating fast, her breath shallow with fear and a sudden crippling feeling of claustrophobia.

"I strongly doubt we can leave."

"You haven't even tried. You're stronger than me. Try to reach the door," she said.

He took a breath, as if he were about to say something and then shrugged. "What the hell. It won't work, but the sooner we get on the same page, the better."

He went to the door and reached for it. His hand stopped. For just a moment, the barest flicker, she thought there was a waver in the barrier. A shimmer in its filmy surface, and within it, a long, wavering shadow with the head of a snake.

Emma's pulse quickened.

"Harder. I think I saw something."

He shot her an indecipherable look. He focused his attention, muttering under his breath, and if she didn't know any better, she'd say he was speaking some sort of spell or incantation.

His hand pressed against the barrier hard, hard enough for him to shift his stance, moving his weight forward. And then his arm flexed, continuing to push as he chanted something.

The whole wall rippled, snake-like figures writhing in its depths and there was a sudden whooshing sound, and objects flying past her in a silver-and-brown blur.

Knives.

Robert fell to his knees, the knives from the kitchen

block—including the one Emma had left on the bed, protruding from his back.

She was frozen, clutching the table and watched in horror as Robert's blood poured to the floor.

For a bare moment, there was incomprehension. Knives didn't just come from nowhere and stab someone. She turned around, expecting to see someone or something, but there was nothing. Robert groaned and she jerked into action, dashing toward him and falling to the floor beside him.

"Pull them out," he said, voice low with pain, his teeth gritted.

"You'll bleed out if I do that."

"No, I won't. I'll heal," he said. "Trust me. Pull them out. The back. Fucking perfect."

Her hand hovered over one of the knives, shaking badly. Pull it out? It would kill him, it had to.

"Emma, stop hesitating and do it," he demanded, his voice laced with authoritative power.

She pulled out the blade, stunned at her own actions. She hadn't meant to do that.

His shirt was soaked with dark crimson. A quick surge of dark blood seeped from the wound and then, stopped. Was he dead? Was that why the blood had slowed so dramatically?

But the tear in his skin was disappearing, pulling together before her very eyes.

Impossible.

"See? I'll be fine. Now do the rest."

A heavy, metallic smell surrounded them. Perhaps it was the stress, or some combination of fear and confusion, but she couldn't think about it anymore. He wanted the knives out, fine. She pulled them out, setting them beside his body. Six knives. All from the butcher block in the kitchen.

He lay on the floor, eyes closed, mouth open as he breathed shallowly. A long moment went by, the sound of crickets coming in from outside. He pushed himself up, sitting up slowly.

"You're healed," she said. Her throat was dry.

"I am," he said. "But at a cost." His accent was different.

"Where are you from?" she asked.

He gave her a long look from under his lashes. "Is that the most relevant question right now?"

"No. But I want to know."

"France. But I've been here a long time. I like to reinvent myself from time to time."

"And you've chosen an American real estate agent?" she asked, feeling sick. There was blood everywhere.

"Not real estate. Remember? Paranormal investigation."

"Like voodoo and witches," she murmured.

"And vampires."

"I don't understand," she said.

"I healed mortal wounds, Emma. I go around covered in the daylight and with a parasol. I required you to invite me in."

"You didn't eat dinner," she said, her gaze searching his face. She wasn't sure how serious he was. He might laugh at her in a moment for believing something so ridiculous. He held her gaze. He didn't laugh.

"I won't harm you. I'm here to help."

"What attacked us?"

"The spirits. We need to find your aunt's altar."

She was about to protest. She'd looked everywhere and there was nowhere it could be. No space large enough for such a thing. Her eyes tracked a drop of blood next to his hand which rested on the floor, propping him up.

The drop slid away from him and made its way across the floor, as if it were sliding down a surface or alive and in a hurry. Another drop followed it, joining with another and another until there were long lines of blood going toward the wall. And then up it.

She got to her feet and pulled hard on his arm to get him up and away from the shrinking pool of blood. He stumbled with her to the other side of the room, leaning heavily on her as they watched the blood slide to the wall, up the wall and into the ceiling.

And then, it was gone. There wasn't a trace left anywhere except what was on his clothes and hers.

"What the hell?" she asked, wondering if perhaps she was hallucinating. Or dreaming this entire experience. Maybe she'd wake up and still be on the plane or be asleep on Dot's bed. Fanciful thinking. Somehow, this was real. And the man next to her, tall and heavy, was more than a man. A vampire. Who'd lost a hell of a lot of blood.

She turned to look at him, caught him staring hungrily at her neck. He shoved away from her. "You don't need to fear me, Emma. I'm hungry, but I can control myself. For a while, at least. We need to get out of here. As soon as possible."

"Yeah, I said that already. And you didn't seem too concerned about us leaving. I guess that's changed, huh? Now that you're... hungry."

"I've lived a long time, Emma. And it's been many decades since I killed someone. Besides, I'm too tired to attack you. Find the altar," he said, and stumbled to the couch. His eyes were sliding shut.

"Don't you go to sleep," she said. "I need you to help me."

"Just a minute..." he murmured.

Emma took a deep breath and paced the room, trying to come up with a plan. Okay. This was Emma in her big-girl pants time. Voodoo was real. Vampires were real. They were trapped here.

"You didn't think I'd make it to morning. That's what you said. Why?"

It took him long moments to answer, as if gathering the energy to speak was difficult. She needed him stronger than this.

"I've seen the movies and read the books. You need blood. If I give you my some of mine, can you help get us out of here?"

"Yes."

"And you won't kill me?" she asked. Wow. Now there was a sentence she'd never wanted or expected to say aloud.

"Promise," he whispered, like a man half-asleep.

Her heart thumped in fear. She'd have to get closer to him.

"Right. Well... here you go," she said, awkwardly holding out her arm toward him.

"Come closer, Emma. It only hurts for a moment."

She stepped warily closer. "And then, what's it like?"

Orgasmic and/or pleasurable would be good answers. Because, despite all of this, he was attractive and the idea of doing something sexual would, under less-terrifying circumstances, be something Emma might really be on board with.

She sank to her knees beside the couch, figuring she better help him out a bit as he seemed so weak. His hand rose, his fingers sliding through hers like a lover. His eyes were bright, hypnotizing almost and the panic she felt about feeding him dimmed, like turning down the volume of a radio. It just wasn't important. Not right now. She felt his breath against her wrist and then the soft brush of his lips.

"Is this vampire foreplay?" she asked.

He smiled. "It depends on how much you like it."

"You can call it foreplay," she said, shifting her weight closer toward him. His teeth grazed the delicate skin of her arm and then there was a flash of sharp, hot pain as his teeth bit into her. As quickly as the pain manifested, it disappeared, replaced by a glorious warmth, better than sunshine or a nice hot bath on a cold day. The pleasure that stole through her was melting, all encompassing. She didn't know how much time passed, didn't care. Her body responded to the sucking of his mouth, pulsing in time to the flow of her blood as it left her and entered him.

The thrill of it grew, became almost too much and then she shattered, crying out in unexpected release.

Her forehead dropped, resting on his firm shoulder. With his tongue, he licked the wound and she felt her skin healing under it, an odd sensation, like an ephemeral zipper gliding across her wrist.

"I need a moment," he said.

She sat up, feeling energized. "Shouldn't I be the one who needs to recover?" she asked.

"You feel all right, then?"

"Better than all right. That's usually how it is for me," she said, blushing. "I, um... come, and then, I'm all energized. Ready to tidy the house or go to the gym." The moment she said it, she wished she could take it back. There was nothing sexy about tidying the house.

She looked down at him, his eyes closed, his breathing

even. She looked down the long, lean length of his body, her gaze snagging at the obvious bulge between his thighs.

Well. That was flattering, at least.

"How big is the altar?" she asked, unsure what it would look like or where such a thing might be hidden.

"A low table, usually. With things on it. Look for something that stands out."

"I don't know where to start."

Emma looked around.

The blood running up the walls was the only clue they had. So, what was upstairs that she hadn't seen yet?

She looked up. Of course. An attic. It hadn't occurred to her to see if there was one yet, but an old house like this would have to have one.

She dashed up the stairs, and there, in the ceiling was a square of wood paneling which had to be some kind of roof access. A large metal handle was attached to the wall to her left. She grabbed hold of it, hauling it down with all her strength until the panel fell open, releasing a cloud of dust. After that, a flaking metal staircase creaked down from the black hole in the ceiling.

Good. Except she had to go up there. Alone.

Emma threw back her shoulders and took the stairs up to the pitch blackness. The place smelled of old books and dried flowers. Nothing seemed to be moving or breathing or about to attack her up there, although until she could actually see anything—it was impossible to tell.

She made her way carefully back down the rusting stairs again to fetch a flashlight. The kitchen didn't have anything and fearing she was running out of time, she brought up a candle in a long candlestick. The flame threw a flickering beam over a dusty, shadowy space full of broken furniture, beads, photograph albums, boxes, old clothes, and alarmingly, hundreds of tiny dolls made of straw and wrapped in bright fabric.

Disturbing as it was, she had to sift through everything. She spent the next hour moving boxes and lifting up coats which sent waves of dust into her eyes and made her sneeze.

The dolls had eyes which seemed to stare at her, as if she had no right to be there. Which she didn't. She should be at home, feet up, watching TV with her dog snoring peacefully beside her.

Eventually, at the back of the room, she found a low wooden table. On it was a statue of a woman kneeling beside a writhing snake, her lips painted a shocking crimson. Above this, pinned to the wall, was a copy of the painting showing the woman dancing with a snake. Someone had scrawled *Maîtresse Brigitte* across it with a red crayon.

This had to be it. The altar. Emma almost shouted with relief.

As well as a collection of burned-down candles, coins, straw dolls and shot glasses, there was a battered old notebook laid out in front of the statue.

More than anything else, the notebook seemed out of place. Unusual. She took it, blew dust off the cover and opened it to find pages and pages written in Dorothy's elegant script.

She put the candle down, and sat cross-legged on a small, round rug in front of the altar. The book was full of lists of herbs, chants and descriptions of rituals—including graphic sketches.

And after reading for a while, she knew what she had to do.

OUTSIDE THE BEDROOM DOOR, Emma stopped and turned to face Robert. He swayed a little, his face still pale but flushed as if he had been running. Her wrist, at the place where he had bitten her, and let's face it, *drank her blood*—throbbed. Her throat went dry and a flash of fear went through her. Followed by anger. Whatever she'd gotten herself into, it was way past her comfort zone. But then he caught her eye and she saw something in his gaze, something she felt herself responding to. A rich stream of emotion. Deep and old and sad and full of anticipation.

He wanted her. And they were in this together.

"We can do this," he said.

"I don't usually sleep with a man on the first date."

"This isn't a date. It's life or death."

"Okay. Well, I don't usually sleep with a guy to break a life-or-death voodoo curse."

He smiled. "You're not doing anything you don't want to do, Emma."

He reached out and ran his hand over the bare skin of her arm and she trembled.

"I never do," she said.

Robert picked up a bundle of dried sage from a rosewood table in the dimly lit hallway, flicked the lid on a Zippo and set fire to it.

Only when the flame died down and the musky smoke surrounded her did she realize she'd been holding her breath.

The heady scent made it seem as though she was outside in the hot, misty, Louisiana night. In fact, as Robert began mumbling a low incantation, calling upon the most revered and beloved Maîtresse Brigitte to appear so that her spirit might enter the willing servant before her, Emma saw movement in the shadows all around. Gasping, she watched as gnarled branches of moss-draped cypress trees began curling out of the walls.

She laughed nervously. This whole voodoo thing was getting way too surreal.

He stepped toward her and tied a velvet blindfold round her head. Emma put her hands over the fabric as her eyes got used to the darkness. Her heart thundered in her chest and she felt Robert's lips on her mouth for a long, lingering moment. He tasted clean, and he was close, so close, and moving his body against hers, strong and male.

"Trust me," he said pulling away, brushing a lock of her hair behind her ear.

"I don't have much choice."

"I won't hurt you."

"If you do, I'll make sure you never work in real estate again."

Emma's hand flew to her injured wrist. Her head was swimming, whether from loss of blood or fear of what was to come, she didn't know. All she could be sure of was that he had fed on her, but she was still alive. What more could she hope for under the circumstances? Sex with him could hardly be worse than dying. In fact, truth be told, every part of her longed for him. Longed to feel again the sensation building as he wove that magic of his into the deepest layers of her.

"I trust you," she said. And her voice sounded strange, as if it didn't belong to her.

"I'm going to undress you now."

Whatever was going to happen, it was too late now. And she wanted him, whether it would break the curse or not. This was real.

She felt his hands unbuttoning her blouse, slipping it over her shoulders. Then unhooking her bra with expert ease, and quickly shucking her skirt down over her hips. Finally, with a sigh, her legs slick with sweat, he slid her panties to her feet and she put a hand on his shoulder as she stepped out of them. The air was cool on her skin.

That was when she started shaking.

Robert took Emma's hand and led her into the room.

"You can take off the blindfold now."

Emma hesitated. Back home, she didn't do kinky stuff. Never had. She had no idea what to expect, but she was pretty sure things were about to get even weirder. She untied the blindfold and blinked in the light of what must have been fifty or more candles burning in the room.

The smoke from a bunch of incense sticks stung her eyes. Rhythmic drumming filled the room, although she couldn't work out where it was coming from. Electricity was down—so who was playing? She guessed it didn't matter and she probably didn't want to know. An image of a ghostly drummer in a black top hat with a cigar rammed between his teeth came to mind. She shook her head. She had to stay focused.

Then she saw him.

Robert was naked, stretched out on the black silk sheets of the bed with Dot's journal open beside him. For a while, Emma ran her eyes over his body, appreciating the landscape of his surprisingly athletic contours. He was broad in the chest, his skin pale, his legs lean.

And he was ready for her.

Then her gaze strayed to what she had thought was a dark bolster lined up alongside his right thigh. Then it moved, undulating. When it shifted slightly into the light and raised its head, she saw what it was and her blood chilled.

The thing had to be about six feet in length. Its tongue

flicked in and out as it seemed to grow more solid with each passing moment.

Robert smiled. "This is the snake spirit they call Le Grande Zombie. It's both male and female, but it only likes to dance with a woman. Pick it up, like in the picture, hold it above your head."

"You want me to touch it?" She didn't think she could.

A hissing sound reverberated round the room. It insinuated itself into her mind and she put her hands over her ears to block it out, but it was impossible.

"What's that noise?" she said.

"You mean the drums?"

"Not that. The other thing. It's so loud. Like you know, a giant snake is shouting at me."

"That's a good sign."

"Of what?"

"He's calling you. You're lucky. You're listening to the song of the great serpent, the python god and goddess combined. Say his name. Ayida. Chikangombe. Monyoha. Welcome him. He is Le Grande Zombie," Robert said, as the snake rose up and slithered toward her.

Emma repeated the names and at last, the room fell silent.

"He's called you to the dance. He sees your beauty and when you take hold of him, Maîtresse Brigitte will enter your body."

An image of the painting downstairs came into her mind. Emma stepped up to the end of the great bed, trembling. "I'm scared."

"Don't be afraid," a deep silky voice in her head told her. "I am the primal spark, the act of love. I am the sky and the waters within you."

Without meaning to, she reached out and touched the

python, just behind its head. A rush of energy raced through her and she felt compelled to lift the snake above her head, taking it in both hands as the drums started up again, beating out a soft, sensuous rhythm.

EMMA DANCED. She took the snake in both hands, lifted it over her head, closed her eyes and moved. At first, it was awkward. Her hips swung side to side, her legs lifting and falling heavily on the plush carpet.

"Don't fight it," Robert said.

She took a deep breath, her heart pulsing in time to the drums. Shifting her attention to this beat, the movements became natural. As natural as breathing. Or fucking.

She stepped onto the bed, one foot on either side of Robert's thighs and she didn't care that she was naked and she didn't really know this man, and that she was undulating like an ancient temple dancer with a six-foot-long snake—a snake which felt so heavy and powerful as she held it high above her.

She was still herself. And yet, she was more than she'd ever been. A sudden jolt of pleasure ran from the top of her head through to the base of her spine, and it seemed as though a golden light wrapped itself round every layer of her.

Robert was chanting words in a strange, guttural language, his voice deep and sonorous. The effect was hypnotic, and she felt a blaze of need rising in her as she threw back her head to find the snake was no longer there.

"Come to me," he said. "Now."

She sank down, knees on either side of him, feeling the cool spark of him against her skin.

She lay her length on top of him, the lines between them blurring as she continued a leisurely version of the dance. She turned her head, placing her cheek against his, whispering her secrets to him—the thrill of it as much a part of the ritual as anything.

When she kissed his face, his jaw, his throat, she heard him groan. This must be what it was like if love could make love to itself.

He put his hands on her hips and she eased him inside, suddenly wanting a primal mating.

The light in the room dimmed as all the candles blew out simultaneously and they were plunged into darkness.

"Slow down," he said, his breath rasping. "She isn't ready yet."

Emma sat up, straddling him. "I am your queen," she said with a voice which wasn't hers.

"You are my queen."

She recalled these words written in the journal, yet, had no idea how she'd managed to remember to say them in the middle of it all.

She threw back her head. "I rule you."

"You rule over me as night rules the stars."

Slowly, she rocked against him, her body serpentine, fluid. He took handfuls of her hair in his fists, rising up until their hearts were pressed together, her arms around his back as he matched her moves. Her peak was long—a series of expanding intensity, igniting fires, rocking her so hard, he had to hold her down, wrenching her to him, leaving her screaming.

Every candle in the room sparked with a new flame. Emma felt herself drifting as the drums faded.

He held her, smoothed her damp hair. "It's done," he said.

———

EMMA MACKENZIE STEPPED out of the French windows into the courtyard of the house on Bourbon Street. The sultry New Orleans night closed around her. A ribbon of moonlight streamed across the cobblestones, casting silver edges on the leaves of palm trees, climbing jasmine and pots of wild, unruly plants she didn't know the names of. The air was a heady mix of perfume and incense. She pulled the dressing gown tight, her skin and hair still wet from the shower. Her body hummed with the extreme pleasure of the ritual.

She imagined telling her mother about what she'd done in the house. *A lot of cleaning up. Dotty Dot left a big mess behind and it turns out she collected dolls. I know. Dolls. Who'd have thought?*

What else could she say? It was not as though she could ever actually tell anybody the truth.

Robert came up behind her, his bare feet padding on the linoleum before stepping outside to join her.

"I've made you some tea," he said.

She turned. He looked immaculate in a white shirt, dark pants. He handed her a cup and smiled in that knowing way he had.

"Do you know a real estate agent?" she said.

"As it happens, I do."

They stood for a while in the night, listening to the sounds of the city as it slumbered. He put his arm around her waist and she closed her eyes, thinking of the river, the wide Mississippi. How it had so much life, so many secrets hidden in its green depths.

"Also, I need a house clearance agency," she said.

"For an estate sale," he said.

She nodded. "I don't feel like going through everything. They can let me have the photographs for the family archives. That's all my mother wants. I should be able to fly home in a couple of days."

There was a long pause.

"I haven't been back to Europe in a few centuries," Robert said.

Emma smiled.

ABOUT THE AUTHORS

Caroline Hanson

Caroline Hanson has written numerous books and is generally considered to be awesome.

Jill Harris

Jill Harris writes fiction and non-fiction. She lives in the New Forest, Hampshire, UK. The forest is actually really old. She's loved stories for as long as she can remember and enjoys nothing more than walking in the woods with her dog dreaming up fabulous characters and strange new worlds. The experience of Authors on a Train was the most amazing thing she's ever done, apart from that time when she lived on a beach in West Africa for a year.

https://jillharrisbooks.org/

Thanks for supporting "Authors on a Train" by purchasing this collection.

If you have a moment, a review would be greatly appreciated.

For more information, go to http://authorsonatrain.com